For my mom.
Thank you for encouraging me
to follow my own road.

ORCA
YOUNG
READERS

Road Block

YOLANDA RIDGE

ORCA BOOK PUBLISHERS

Library and Archives Canada Cataloguing in Publication

Ridge, Yolanda, 1973-
Road block / Yolanda Ridge.
(Orca young readers)

Issued also in electronic formats.
ISBN 978-1-4598-0045-8

I. Title. II. Series: Orca young readers
PS8635.I374R62 2012   JC813'.6   C2011-907763-9

First published in the United States, 2012
Library of Congress Control Number: 2011943719

Summary: Bree tries to stop a highway development in rural Ontario, but her own family stands in her way.

MIX
Paper from
responsible sources
FSC
www.fsc.org   **FSC® C004071**

Orca Book Publishers is dedicated to preserving the environment and has printed this book on paper certified by the Forest Stewardship Council®.

Orca Book Publishers gratefully acknowledges the support for its publishing programs provided by the following agencies: the Government of Canada through the Canada Book Fund and the Canada Council for the Arts, and the Province of British Columbia through the BC Arts Council and the Book Publishing Tax Credit.

Cover artwork by Peter Ferguson
Author photo by Tim Ridge

ORCA BOOK PUBLISHERS
PO Box 5626, Stn. B
Victoria, BC Canada
V8R 6S4

ORCA BOOK PUBLISHERS
PO Box 468
Custer, WA USA
98240-0468

www.orcabook.com
Printed and bound in Canada.

15 14 13 12 • 4 3 2 1

Chapter One

When the bell rang at the end of the day, I ran for home, and I didn't slow down until I reached the front entrance of my townhouse complex. As I walked through Cedar Grove, I looked around. Where was everyone? I wanted to celebrate!

It was the last day of school, and I had lots to be excited about. Grade six was over. Done. No more classes, no more homework, no more exams—not for another two months anyway. And I planned to make the most of my summer: climbing, swimming, hanging out with my friends…oh, and earning a bit of money by helping Ms. Matheson clean up after their kitchen renovation. Her son, Ethan, and I were saving up to take a climbing course through Tree Climbers International.

I barged into my townhouse, letting the door slam shut behind me.

"Bree?"

Startled by the sound of my name, I spun around. "Dad?"

"In the kitchen."

I threw my backpack toward the bottom of the stairs and headed down the hall. I was surprised Dad was home. He'd cancelled our usual last-day-of-school celebration at Main Street Gelato because of some big meeting at work. He'd had a lot of those lately, which was weird. Hockey scouts aren't usually that busy during the summer, so Dad and I hang out while Mom's at work.

"What are you doing here?" I asked.

"I need to talk to you, sweetie," Dad said, wiping his hands on an apron that said *Eat, Sleep and Play Hockey.*

Sweetie? This couldn't be good. Dad never used lovey-dovey nicknames unless something was up. Something bad.

"Now? I was hoping to go climbing. With Ethan and Michael." I lowered my head so Dad wouldn't see me blush when I said Michael's name.

"It won't take long. I made some brownies."

My head shot up along with my eyebrows. First *sweetie* and now brownies. Dad was a good cook, but baking? "What's going on, Dad?"

"Well, I've got some news to share with you," Dad said.

"What is it?" I asked.

"Have a seat out back, and I'll bring the snacks," Dad said.

I was beyond curious, but I knew there was no point rushing him. He was always slow choosing his words. Mom said it was from years of dealing with difficult people. I assumed she meant hockey players, who she often referred to as hotheads.

I went out through the sliding glass door and sat down at the picnic table that took up most of our postage stamp of a backyard. Seconds later, Dad came out with a plate of brownies and two glasses of milk. "It's not gelato, but…"

"Come on, Dad. Spill it. What's the news?"

Dad sat down on the bench across from me. "I've got a new job."

"You're leaving the Canucks?"

"No, no. Actually, the Canucks gave me a promotion," Dad said, not sounding nearly as happy as he should.

I'd heard him tell Mom lots of times that hockey scouts don't get promoted very often.

"A promotion? That's great, Dad!"

"Yes, it's exciting," he said, still not sounding excited. "Next season, I'll be managing the other professional scouts, including whoever I hire to fill my old position. But first I need to spend some time in Europe, dealing with immigration issues for the current Canucks players and their families."

"That's great!" I said again. "You love Europe."

"Yes, I'm going to Europe," Dad said. Then he paused and looked at me through narrowed eyes, as if he were trying to read my mind. "This summer."

"So we're going on a summer vacation? To Europe?" I knew I was missing something, but I hadn't put it together yet.

"I'll be gone for two months. And Mom has to work all summer on that new development in False Creek. She won't have any vacation days until the fall."

I looked at Dad. I looked at the table. Neither of us had touched the brownies. Or the milk. I took a deep breath. My brain was catching up. "What about me?"

"Your mom and I want you to spend the summer with Grandma."

"In Ontario?" I croaked, my mouth suddenly dry.

"Yes, at the farm."

"No," I said, without raising my eyes from the table. I knew that if I looked at Dad I'd start to cry. "No."

"I'm sorry, Bree."

I swallowed hard. "But what about our summer in Vancouver? What about Kits Beach? Splashdown Park? The Festival of Lights? The roller coasters at Playland... the PNE! All the stuff we were going to do together!"

"That was when I had the summer off. I was excited about all that too."

"Then don't go," I begged. "What kind of promotion is it anyway, if they make you work all summer?"

"Well, it's more money," Dad said, finally taking a brownie from the plate. "But more importantly, as Director of Hockey Administration, I won't have to scout as many games. Probably less than ten per month, instead of twenty-five or more."

"But you have to do other stuff. Like spending the summer in Europe. Without me."

"Yes. But I'll be spending a lot less time traveling to all those small towns during the season. This way I'll be here for you more, you know, during the school year." Dad gave me a half smile, the fake kind that showed no teeth or dimples, and took a bite of brownie.

I wanted to be happy for him. I really did. But spending the summer in Ontario? That would be bad.

"Can't I just stay here? With Mom?"

"Mom's going to be logging a lot of overtime hours this summer to meet her deadlines. Neither of us think it would be good for you to spend so much time on your own."

"But I wouldn't be alone. All my friends will be here."

"You know Sarah's spending most of the summer in Surrey," Dad said. Sarah was my best friend. Her mom lived in a huge house in the suburbs with her new husband and his kids. During the school year, Sarah lived with her dad in the townhouse complex next to Cedar Grove.

"I have other friends," I protested.

"I've talked to the other Cedar Grove parents," Dad said, "and no one's going to be here much. Michael's going to hockey camp, Ashley's taking art classes at Emily Carr—"

"Ethan will be around," I interrupted. "His mom's going to pay us to do a bunch of clean-up and stuff. She'll keep an eye on us, that's for sure."

"Your grandma could use the company," Dad said.

"Why does she need *my* company?" I said, pulling myself to the edge of the bench. "The whole rest of the family is there. Right next door."

"She could use your help. Things are complicated on the farm right now." Dad took another bite of brownie and chewed. Slowly.

"Complicated how?"

Dad swallowed. "Well, it looks like the highway construction is finally going ahead."

"Really?" There'd been talk about building a highway through my grandma's farmland for, well, forever. But no one thought it would actually happen.

"Really. This could be your last chance to spend time there."

"But I don't want to spend any time there," I said, looking closer at Dad. He looked so calm and I felt so...NOT calm.

"I'm sorry, Bree," Dad repeated. "But Mom has already booked your plane ticket. You leave Monday. Same day as me."

"I can't believe you booked my ticket without talking to me first!" The risk of crying had passed. I was way, way too angry for tears. I picked up my milk to take a sip but changed my mind and slammed it back down on the picnic table. I watched as the milk splashed over the side of the glass, leaving a small white pond on the wood. "Where's Mom anyway? Why isn't she here helping you share this *wonderful* news with me?"

"We thought you might take it better if it came from me," Dad said.

"Well, you were wrong. Nothing could make this better!"

"It might be fun, Bree. There's lots of space on the farm. Lots of trees to climb."

"But I want to climb here. It's what I fought for. What we all fought for." It had been less than a month since the bylaw against tree climbing in Cedar Grove had been overturned. I couldn't believe it. All that hard work and I wasn't even going to be able to enjoy it!

"I'm sorry, Bree," Dad said again.

"Me too," I said, jumping to my feet. I couldn't sit still any longer. Ethan and Michael would be waiting for me. We had trees to climb.

"There's still time for some fun before we leave…"

I didn't stick around to listen to the rest of what Dad had to say. Stepping into the house, I slid the door shut behind me. Hard. A lot harder than necessary. My way of getting the last word.

Not that it made me feel any better.

Chapter Two

Five days later I was sitting in the farmhouse with Grandma, drinking juice and eating donuts. The donuts were dry and disgusting, but I was inhaling them anyway. The six-hour trip from Vancouver to Waterloo International Airport had given me an appetite. And judging by the empty cans and foil dinner trays littering the kitchen counter, I wasn't getting a home-cooked, country-style meal anytime soon.

"Didn't they feed you on the plane, Brianna?" Grandma asked.

"Just some cookies and pretzels," I replied, fighting the urge to roll my eyes. I'd already told her every detail of the flight on the short drive from the airport to the farm. And really, there hadn't been much to tell.

The biggest surprise of the trip so far was how close the new airport was to the farm. Waterloo International Airport was actually in Breslau, my dad's hometown. Right in the middle of nowhere. Surrounded by nothing but flat fields and farmhouses.

"We'll have soup for dinner," Grandma said. "I stocked up at Walmart when they had a case lot sale."

"Okay," I replied.

There was an uncomfortable silence. Like it was obvious to both of us that we'd already used up all possible topics of conversation in the short time since I'd arrived.

"Is it okay if I use the bathroom?"

"Of course," Grandma said. "You know where it is?"

"Yup." How could I forget the bathroom on the farm? The drip of water that passed for a shower. The rattling of pipes every time you turned on a tap. The sign above the toilet that read *If you sprinkle when you tinkle, please be sweet and wipe the seat.* Gross.

When I returned to the kitchen, Grandma was knitting.

"What are you making?" I asked, pointing to the soft blue yarn.

"A hat for the Children's Hospital. They put them on the little babies, the premature ones, to keep them warm."

"Oh," I said.

Another silence.

Where was the rest of the family—my cousins and my uncle? The last time I was at the farm was for my Aunt Theresa's memorial service. That was five years ago. No one seemed to care that I'd finally come back. My friends in Cedar Grove were more excited to see me after a sick day. Not that I had many of those. If I spent a day sick in bed, I missed out on too much fun.

Thinking of home, I pulled out the iPhone Dad had given me at the airport. To help us keep in touch, he'd said. And to make him feel a little less guilty about abandoning his only child for the summer, I thought.

"What's that?" Grandma asked.

"An iPhone. I promised Mom I'd let her know when I got here."

"There's a phone right there," Grandma said, pointing to the wall with one of her knitting needles. "What do you need that thing for?"

"To keep in touch with Dad. With my friends. Send texts. Play with apps. Surf the Net." I rattled off the list quickly. "Do you have wireless?"

"What?"

"An Internet connection. You know, for the computer?"

Grandma's knitting needles didn't slow down at all as she looked up at me and answered, "There's no computer here."

"No computer? No Internet?" I said. It wasn't exactly surprising, but for some reason that horrible thought had never occurred to me. Until now. How come it hadn't occurred to Dad? He'd even put Skype on my iPhone so we could call each other for free. Had it really been that long since he visited the farm? So long that he'd forgotten it was like going back to the age of the dinosaurs?

"What do I need a computer for?" Grandma said sharply.

I started randomly pushing buttons. "What about cell-phone reception?" I asked.

"Don't know," Grandma replied. "Why?"

I groaned as my iPhone searched for a connection.

"Maybe Sonny can help you," Grandma said, knitting needles still flying.

My next question was interrupted by a series of high-pitched chimes that sounded like the Gastown steam clock in Vancouver.

"Doorbell," Grandma reported, not moving from her chair.

I jumped up. "I'll get it." I was hoping it was one of my cousins or my uncle or anybody under the age of fifty who might know something about modern technology.

I pulled open the door, almost ripping off the worn-out handle.

"Good afternoon." The man on the other side of the door looked like he might know something about computers. He also looked very out of place in his suit and tie.

"Uh, hi?"

"I'm here to speak with Mrs. Lisette Bridges," the man said.

"You know my grandma?"

"Yes. My name is Percy Murfin. And you are?"

"Bree."

"Hello, Bree. Pleased to meet you." Percy Murfin grabbed my hand and shook it, squeezing so hard I thought my fingers were going to break. Then he asked, "Is your grandmother home?"

"Uh, yes." I paused, unsure whether to invite him in or leave him standing at the door. "Grandma! A man's here to see you!"

Before I had finished yelling, Grandma was standing behind me. "What do you want?" she demanded.

"Good afternoon, Mrs. Bridges," Percy Murfin said smoothly. "I see you have some company. Maybe now is not a good time."

"It's never a good time, Mr. Murfin," Grandma said.

Percy Murfin smiled. "I'd be happy to come back when your granddaughter is gone. When you have more time."

"Brianna's going to be here all summer," Grandma said, placing her hands on my shoulders. It was the first time she'd touched me since I arrived, and I felt more than a little uncomfortable standing there between her and this Percy Murfin guy. "If you've got something to say, make it quick."

"Well, actually I have some paperwork I'd like to go over with you, Mrs. Bridges." Percy Murfin raised his briefcase. "Things are starting to move quickly, and we need your cooperation."

"What things?" I said, looking back at Grandma.

"Mr. Murfin here wants to buy the farm," Grandma said to me. "Our farm."

"It's not me that wants to, Mrs. Bridges," Percy Murfin said. "The province needs this land to build the highway."

"Is there something I need to sign?" Grandma asked.

"Not yet, but we need your—"

Grandma cut him off. "I've already told you Mr. Murfin. When you are ready to build the highway, you can have the land you need. Until then, I don't want to hear about it."

"There's some new information. Including a time-line," Percy Murfin said. He opened his briefcase and started to dig.

"Doesn't matter," Grandma said.

"But, Grandma, what if it's something important?" I asked.

"It's not," Grandma said, pushing down on my shoulders. "They've been planning this darn highway for ten, maybe twenty, years now. I don't want to talk about it unless it's actually going to happen."

"It's getting close now, Mrs. Bridges." Percy Murfin held out a piece of paper. "There's going to be an information meeting next Wednesday night. It would be great if you could come. We're hoping to get lots of input from local residents. It's really important to us that we minimize the impact of this construction as much as possible."

Behind me, I heard Grandma snort. Loudly.

"Grandma," I said quickly, "I think we should go."

"Waste of time," Grandma said.

"But it could be important," I insisted, taking the piece of paper from Percy Murfin. Was this what Dad was talking about when he said Grandma could use my help? I had thought he meant weeding the garden, stacking wood for winter, keeping her company while she made jam…stuff like that. Could he have been talking about something much more important?

"Not important," Grandma said. "Good day, Mr. Murfin."

And with that, she slammed the door in his face.

Chapter Three

I sat on a branch halfway up the tree with my back against the trunk and my legs stretched out in front of me. It felt great to be outside. The air was so fresh here. Like the produce stalls at the East Vancouver Farmer's Market, but without the lingering smell of hot asphalt from the parking lot.

I'd escaped the farmhouse immediately after Grandma slammed the door on Percy Murfin. She'd gone back to her knitting as if nothing had happened and seemed more than a little relieved when I'd said I was going outside.

It hadn't taken me long to find the tree I was sitting in, which I named Gnarly as soon as I saw it. It was twisted and old and difficult to climb. It was going to take some planning to get to the top, but I'd reached this spot quite easily. The farm was so flat that I could see a lot already, including Percy Murfin's shiny black car at the end of the long lane, signal light blinking, still waiting to turn left onto the busy road.

I pulled out the notice he'd brought for Grandma but had given to me.

New Highway 7 Alignment Project:
Information Meeting
Rerouting of the heavily traveled east-west highway connecting Guelph and Kitchener has been in the planning stages for some time. Environmental assessments and surveying for this project have now been completed. Detailed maps, land acquisition information and proposed timelines for the project will be available for public review on
Wednesday, July 13, from 6:30–8:30 PM
Kitchener Public Library, 85 Queen St. North

"Hello?"

The voice startled me, and I dropped the notice. I watched as it floated down and landed at the feet of a guy I didn't recognize.

He was looking up at me through the leaves. "Bree?"

"Who are you?" I asked, wondering whether he was a trespasser or a family friend. But a trespasser wouldn't know my name. The whole Percy Murfin thing had put me on edge.

"It's me. Sonny. Grandma said you were back here somewhere."

Sonny? My cousin Sonny? Five years ago he was a short, nerdy nine-year-old. Now he looked like one of those teenagers that hang out at the local mall in baseball hats and baggy jeans. "Really?"

"What are you doing up there?" he asked.

"Nothing."

"Can I come up?"

"I guess."

I watched as Sonny climbed into the tree without hesitation. It was hard to believe he was the same person who'd convinced me that he could receive alien signals through the bug zapper on Grandma and Grandpa's front porch. That was when we were little, of course, and he used to play tricks on me all the time. When I was seven, he'd seemed like the smartest kid I'd ever met.

Within minutes he was sitting comfortably on the branch next to me.

"You climb?" I said, unable to hide my surprise. The cousin I remembered wasn't exactly the tree-climbing type.

"Yeah, I guess," Sonny said, pursing his lips together. "I don't know of any other way to get up into a tree."

"You like trees?"

"I like that no one can find me up here."

"Oh," I said. Maybe Sonny and I were more alike than I thought.

"I hear you have an iPhone," Sonny said, breaking the silence that had settled between us.

"Where'd you hear that?"

Sonny started to respond, but he was drowned out by the noise of a jet flying over us. "Where is it?" he asked when the airplane had passed.

"The iPhone? I left it inside. I couldn't get it to work. No signal out here, I guess."

"Bring it to dinner," Sonny said. "I'll have a look at it for you."

"Dinner?"

"Yup, Amber's cooking." Amber was Sonny's twin sister. But the only thing they had in common was their birthday. At least that's what I remembered.

"Grandma's planning on making soup," I said.

"Yeah, well, you won't get any canned soup at our place," Sonny said. "Amber wants us to try and make you feel welcome."

"That's nice," I said, wondering how hard they would have to try.

"You might not think so after you've eaten," Sonny said as he reached for the trunk of the tree and stepped onto the branch below him.

I sat in the tree while Sonny climbed down and jumped from a branch that seemed too high. Too high for me to jump from, that's for sure. But Sonny was tall. Tall in a freakish beanstalk kind of way.

I followed him to the bottom and picked up the notice at the base of the tree. "Do you know anything about this information meeting?"

"Information meeting?"

"You know, about the highway," I said, handing him the notice.

Sonny glanced at the paper. "Oh, another one of those," he said. "I stopped paying attention to that a long time ago." He crumpled the notice into a ball and threw it at me playfully. It wasn't a good throw, but I caught it anyway.

"They're putting the highway right through your home. Isn't it kind of important?"

"Talk to Dad about it. He's probably going to the meeting," Sonny said over his shoulder as he walked away toward the house at the other end of the cornfield.

There were two houses on the farm: the original farmhouse and a much newer house that was built after Sonny's mom, Aunt Theresa, died. Grandma had insisted that Sonny and his family live on the farm so she could help out. I'm not sure Grandma had been that helpful, but I guess it made sense at the time. Sonny and Amber's younger brother, Jasper, had been a baby when their mom was hit by a car.

Forgetting about the iPhone, I followed Sonny. I was anxious for some company, and I didn't want to face Grandma just yet. "So, what are you growing here?" I asked.

"We're not growing anything," Sonny replied, "not anymore. Everything's done by the big industrial growers now." Sonny slowed down a little and gestured toward the fields. "Those are soybeans. That's corn."

"What's in there?" I asked, pointing to the barn. Its faded, peeling paint made it look pink in the evening sun.

"Grandma rents that out too. It's full of old restaurant equipment."

"Oh," I said, feeling disappointed. As I walked around the farm, I remembered the animals I had seen there when I was a little kid. The pigs and the barn cats. The horses and the cows. There was even a pony. Grandpa let me ride it once.

When we got to Sonny's house, we were greeted by a small flock of chickens. "Are these rented as well?" I asked.

Sonny laughed as he chased a big brown one away from the front door. "These girls belong to Amber and me."

"Oh good." I laughed as another chicken started pecking at Sonny's shoelace.

Sonny opened the door. "You go in and say hi. I'm gonna do a bit of work out here."

"Okay. Thanks." I stepped inside and followed the noise to the kitchen where I found Amber bent over the stove. Jasper was sitting at her feet, playing with trucks. Neither of them looked up as I walked into the room.

"There you are, Bree," Grandma said. She was sitting at the table with her knitting.

"Bree!" Amber turned from the stove and walked over to give me a hug. She was a lot shorter than Sonny and looked pretty normal. Except maybe for the shirt she was wearing, which had sleeves made of different colored fabrics with symbols I didn't recognize printed on the front. "It's good to see you."

"It's good to see you too," I said as we exchanged a quick hug. "Thanks for cooking."

"Look, Jasper," Amber said, "it's our cousin, Bree."

Jasper stared at me but didn't say a thing.

"He won't recognize her. It's been too long," Grandma said.

"Dinner's almost ready, but we won't be eating until Dad gets home," Amber said, ignoring Grandma as she turned back to the stove.

I sat down on the floor next to Jasper, who had returned to his trucks. "When will that be?" I asked.

"Not too late, I hope," Amber replied. "He knows you're coming, but things have been busy at the office lately."

"What else is new?" Grandma muttered under her breath.

I didn't know much about what my uncle did. Just that it had something to do with numbers and nothing to do with the farm.

By the time Uncle Doug got home, I was beyond starving and bored to death. Amber had continued to putter around the kitchen, finding little things to do even though it was obvious that supper had been ready for over an hour. Grandma knitted. Sonny stayed outside. I sat on the floor and played with Jasper, who was very different from the chatty five-year-olds I knew in Cedar Grove. I had always assumed that noise and little boys went together like peanut butter and jam. Apparently, that wasn't the case. I wondered if this was what Dad meant when he talked about how much Aunt Theresa's death had affected the family.

Dinner was okay but mostly silent. Amber had gone to a lot of effort to create what she described as "a sophisticated dish." Asparagus crepes with a creamy red-pepper sauce. "Like something you might find in Vancouver or New York," she said.

When she asked her dad how he liked it, he said he preferred meatloaf. Amber didn't seem surprised, but I almost choked on my crepe. My dad was always trying to get me to cook with him. And when I did, he was totally enthusiastic and complimentary. He'd probably enjoy eating dog food if I helped him prepare it.

I made sure Amber knew how much I enjoyed her dinner, which was actually pretty good. And I was the only one who helped her clean up afterward.

I didn't get a chance to ask Uncle Doug about the highway information meeting until Grandma and I were about to leave. "Yeah, I'll be going to the meeting," Uncle Doug said with a yawn. "Why?"

"I'd like to go too," I replied, "but Grandma doesn't want to."

Uncle Doug looked surprised. "You want to go? Why? No one round here is very interested in what happens to this farm except me."

"I'm interested," I said.

"Why do you care? Your daddy doesn't."

I felt my cheeks go red. "I don't know."

"Well, you are welcome to come with me as long as you understand that you'll be on your own once we get there. I've got some important matters to discuss with Mr. Murfin."

"Okay, that'd be great, Uncle Doug," I said, feeling a little better. I was glad someone in the family was planning to speak to Percy Murfin about the highway.

It just didn't seem right to put a highway through the farm.

Our farm, as Grandma had called it.

Chapter Four

I was happy when Wednesday finally came. Not because I was particularly excited about spending time with Uncle Doug. And not because I was excited about the information meeting. It was just nice to have something to do.

Something other than gathering eggs in the chicken coop with Jasper every day. Which was actually kind of fun except that it never took very long. I loved the discovery of each fragile oval egg lying in its nest, still warm from the hen who'd abandoned it for her morning feed.

Uncle Doug didn't say much as we drove into Kitchener. I asked a few questions about the highway, but he just answered with a simple "yes" or "no" and didn't provide any extra information. It was hard to believe this was the same uncle I'd celebrated the holidays with when I was younger.

I had one really great memory of Christmas at the farm. Mom, Dad and I had flown in from Vancouver on Christmas Eve to stay with Grandma and Grandpa at the farmhouse. I'd slept in the living room on the green corduroy couch that was so soft and comfy I sank right into its cushions. I was hoping to see Santa so I'd have something really cool to tell my cousins when they arrived in the morning. I didn't see Santa, of course, but when I woke up on Christmas Day, the tree was surrounded by brightly wrapped packages and the ground outside was covered with more snow than I'd ever seen.

Sonny and Amber didn't live on the farm then, and when they arrived, Uncle Doug's truck got stuck in the lane. I remember the thrill I felt as Mom bundled me up and sent me outside with Dad and Grandpa to pull them out with the tractor. It took almost an hour, and it snowed the whole time. It was amazing! And when we finally got the truck up to the farmhouse, we got into a great big snowball fight that had everyone laughing so hard we didn't even feel the cold. I can still see the icicles hanging off Uncle Doug's beard as he pulled Aunt Theresa onto the top of a snowdrift.

When we finally got back inside the farmhouse, Grandma had made hot chocolate, and Grandpa stoked the fire until it was roaring. That was my best Christmas moment ever. And I hadn't even opened a single present.

We got to the meeting just after 6:30. The presentation had already started, so Uncle Doug and I grabbed a seat near the back. There were a lot of empty chairs.

I sat and listened as men in suits, including Percy Murfin, talked about lanes, dividers, shoulders, right-of-ways, overpasses, traffic lights...blah, blah, blah. They also showed a bunch of maps that didn't mean anything to me.

Uncle Doug disappeared as soon as the presentation was over, mumbling something about meeting me back at the truck later.

I wasn't sure what to do. In fact, I was starting to wonder why I was even there. None of this highway business made much sense, and it didn't really matter if I understood it. All that mattered was that my uncle needed to oppose the highway and protect the farm.

I walked around the room, looking at the mixed group of people who'd come to the meeting. Some of the older adults were still sitting in their seats talking quietly. Probably discussing politics, banana bread recipes, the wonderfulness of their grandkids. You know—the stuff grandparents always talk about. Other people closer to Mom and Dad's age were browsing the wall of displays. There were no other kids there. Just me.

I stopped to look at a map labeled *Land Acquistion* that was posted on the wall. The map was marked up with big red lines, making it look like a teacher had given the student who drew it a really bad grade. I was trying to guess which of the boxes that covered the map like a checkerboard was meant to be our farm when one of the older ladies came up and stood beside me. She chewed her lip as she studied the map, adjusting her reading glasses over and over again. She looked as confused as I felt.

"It doesn't make sense to me," I finally said. "Does it make sense to you?"

"Clear as mud," she replied with a frown.

We laughed.

"This highway expansion's got me up a pole," she said. "I don't know whether I'm coming or going."

"You don't like it?"

"Like it? Hah. It's a wolf at my door. Soon there's going to be thousands of cars and trucks roaring past my house at all hours of the day and night."

"You live next to the highway?"

"In Breslau."

"Me too!" I said. "I mean, not me, but my grandma. I'm from Vancouver."

"Then I guess you know all about noise and traffic. What are you doing here?"

"I'm spending the summer with my grandma," I said.

"She here?"

"No. I'm here with my uncle. He lives on the farm too. In Breslau."

"Then I'm guessing you're related to the Bridges."

"Yes, Lisette Bridges is my grandma—" I started.

"And Doug Junior is your uncle," she finished.

"You know them?" I asked.

"Know them? Hah. I've known your grandma for over fifty years. We're neighbors." She held out her hand. "I'm Mrs. Kornitsky."

"Brianna Bridges," I said, feeling her rough fingers curl around my hand. "Everyone calls me Bree."

Instead of shaking my hand, like I thought she would, Mrs. Kornitsky patted it gently with her other hand. "So you belong to Steven," she said.

"He's my dad," I replied.

Mrs. Kornitsky smiled and released my hand. "He used to horse around with my boys all the time. In those days, the kids were out of the house at dawn, playing in the fields and fishing in the streams. Us parents never thought twice unless someone didn't make it home for the evening meal."

"So the highway's going to go through your farmland too?"

"No." Mrs. Kornitsky's voice went flat as her face fell back to a frown. "The highway won't go through my land, it'll go next to it."

"Does that mean you can keep your land? Keep your home?"

"It means the province won't buy it. They won't even give me a dime. Just a noisy new neighbor and a decreased property value."

"You *want* to move?"

"Doesn't matter what I want. No one's going to buy a piece of land that's sandwiched between an airport runway and a superhighway."

"Oh," I said. "That doesn't seem fair. Isn't there something you can do?"

"What's an old lady like me going to do?" Mrs. Kornitsky replied. "You know what they say— you can't fight city hall."

"Maybe you should talk to Per—I mean, Mr. Murfin," I said.

Mrs. Kornitsky peered at me over her glasses and whispered, "Mr. Murfin and the other government lads don't waste their time with me. They just want to get the land they need for as little money as possible."

"There must be something you can do," I said, even though I had no idea what it was.

"I wish there were, Bree." Mrs. Kornitsky took my hand and patted it again. "I wish there were."

I frowned.

Mrs. Kornitsky dropped my hand. "I'm going to make a beeline for the door. Nice to meet you, my dear. You should come round for milk and cookies sometime."

"Thanks," I said, resisting the urge to follow Mrs. Kornitsky home. I was ready to go.

Instead I went in search of Uncle Doug. He was off in the corner, talking to Percy Murfin. They were so involved in their conversation they didn't see me coming. And knowing it would be rude to interrupt, I decided to keep quiet. That's how I ended up over-hearing what they were saying.

"Your mother owns the land. I need her signature. It's as simple as that, Doug," said Percy Murfin.

"Listen, Percy, you know as well as I do that my mom's not qualified to make a big decision like this. She can't negotiate with you. It has to be me," Uncle Doug said.

"Are you trying to tell me that your mother is not of sound mind?"

"If that's what it takes, yes," said Uncle Doug.

"Then you need documentation from a medical doctor," Percy Murfin said, "and you've got to get the lawyers involved. It's called Power of Attorney. You can't do anything without it."

"You really want to wait for us to do that, Percy? The plan is to break ground in the fall." Uncle Doug leaned in toward Percy Murfin and lowered his head.

I took a step closer.

"We're not going to do anything to stop the highway from being built," Uncle Doug said. "Heck, I want it to be built. Sooner rather than later. I'm just asking for a slight change. Route the highway east and you'll only have to buy a portion of the land. It'll save the province money."

"We get a lot of bad publicity when farmland is cut in half. And there are other considerations—"

"You won't get any bad publicity from us," Uncle Doug interrupted, "unless you keep refusing to consider my proposal."

"I understand you want to save whatever you can of your family's land, Doug. But I don't understand why you want a busy highway running past your mother's front door."

"I'm not trying to save the land for my mom. She'll be moving soon enough. Like I said, she needs medical attention." Uncle Doug pointed his finger at the side of his head and drew a couple of circles in the air.

I gasped. My hand flew up to my mouth to cover the noise.

Uncle Doug continued, "I want to develop the land. Make some real money. This province should be supporting businessmen like me!"

"There's no room for negotiation, Doug. The route has been determined. It's within our rights to take the land, start building and compensate your family later. That's what will happen if you pursue this. If you get lawyers involved. Think about how hard that will be on your mother. Especially if she does have some type of mental condition, as you are implying."

Uncle Doug looked up. His face was bright red, and there were little beads of sweat settling between his eyebrows. I wouldn't have been surprised to see steam rising up from the top of his head.

I took another step closer.

Percy Murfin saw me first. "Bree," he said. I was surprised he remembered my name. "It's good to see you again."

"What's going on, Uncle Doug?" I asked.

"Nothing, Brianna," said Uncle Doug, wiping the sweat off his forehead with the back of his hand. He wasn't happy to see me, that's for sure. "Time to go."

"But…" I mumbled, not sure what to say. My tongue felt thick and numb and disconnected from my brain. I wasn't sure what was more shocking: that Uncle Doug didn't want to stop the highway or that he'd called Grandma crazy.

I didn't like the uncle I'd seen since arriving in Ontario, but I'd done my best to give him the benefit of the doubt. I'd tried to convince myself that he was just having a bad day. Okay, ten bad days. In a row. But I just had to believe there was something left of the fun uncle I remembered. Spending the summer with a grumpy grandma and an evil uncle was more than I thought I could handle.

"I'll be in touch," Uncle Doug said to Percy Murfin.

"I'm sure you will," Percy Murfin replied. "I'm sure you will."

"This isn't the end of it," Uncle Doug said over his shoulder as we headed to the door.

But it was the end of something. It was the end of my belief that Uncle Doug would do the right thing.

Chapter Five

It was all very confusing. I knew what I'd heard, but I wasn't sure I knew what it meant. And I didn't want to accuse Uncle Doug of something and be wrong. That would be bad.

I couldn't figure out how to get more information. So all I did was think about it. For days and days. There really wasn't much else to do.

I hardly ever saw Sonny, even though I spent lots of time climbing Gnarly. It was a week after the meeting when I finally found Sonny hanging out in the shade of the barn. He was sitting against the side door with his shirt off and a laptop on his knees. It was a hot day. Hot in that gross humid Ontario way.

"Hey, Sonny," I said.

He shut the laptop and grabbed his shirt. "Hi, Bree."

I sat down on the grass next to him and asked, "What are you doing?"

Sonny lifted the computer back onto his lap. "I get a good signal here."

"You have wireless?"

Sonny nodded. "Dad finally agreed to get it last year because we needed it for school. But he got the cheapest plan possible. This is as far as I can get from the house without losing the connection."

"Can I use it for my iPhone?"

"Sure. I'll set it up for you. Later." Sonny opened his computer. "I'm busy now."

"What are you doing? Sending emails?" I asked.

"Surfing the Net," he replied.

"For…" I prompted. Why was everyone here so hard to talk to?

"Information on organic farming."

"Oh," I said, once again surprised by Sonny. "Why?"

"Why not?"

"I didn't think you were all that interested in the farm."

"What made you think that?"

"Because you don't care about the highway."

"I never said I didn't care."

"But you weren't interested in going to the meeting. You said you'd stopped paying attention."

"Yeah, well, that doesn't mean I don't care. I don't want that stupid highway."

"You don't?"

"No," Sonny said. "I think they should expand the GO Train."

"GO Train?"

"Public transit. A much better way of dealing with the traffic congestion between here and Toronto." Sonny was reading something on the computer as he talked. "Get people out of their cars."

"Makes sense," I said. Why hadn't I thought of that? A rapid transit line had recently been built in Vancouver between the airport and downtown. The traffic around my townhouse complex had jammed up like crazy during the construction, but the roads were much less congested now that the trains were finally running. "Public transit is a good idea. Why don't you speak up about it?"

Sonny looked at me. "You just don't get it, do you?"

"Explain it to me!"

Sonny sighed. Loudly. Like he was thinking things over. Maybe trying to decide what I should know. Or maybe trying to figure out how to get rid of me so he could go back to his computer. Back to learning about organic farming.

"Please," I added in a softer tone, hoping to get something out of him. Anything.

Sonny still wasn't talking, so I filled the silence. "When I was at the meeting, I heard your dad talking to Percy Murfin."

Sonny started typing. "Uh-huh," he said.

"Your dad doesn't want to stop the highway. He told Mr. Murfin that he wants the route changed," I said.

"Uh-huh," Sonny said again.

"So the province only has to buy part of the land and he can…" I hestitated, trying to make sense of what I'd overheard.

"So he can develop the rest," Sonny finished.

"Develop it into what?"

"You know: PetroCan, Tim Hortons, megastores like Costco and Canadian Tire. He says you can make a lot of money leasing land. More than you can farming, that's for sure."

I frowned, trying to imagine that kind of transformation. "At least you wouldn't have to move," I said.

"But we would." Sonny looked up from his computer. His eyes seemed to search the land around us, stopping briefly on his house in the distance. "As soon as Dad makes a bit of money, we're out of here."

"And Grandma? He told Mr. Murfin that she'll be moving soon."

"He's looking at those retirement homes. The ones for old folks," Sonny said. "The flyers have been coming in the mail."

I inhaled sharply, like I'd just been hit in the stomach. Uncle Doug really did think Grandma was crazy! When I was breathing again, I asked, "Does Grandma know?"

"I doubt it," Sonny replied. "They don't talk much."

"I think Grandma wants to stay on the farm. Don't you? This is her home."

Sonny shrugged. Then he closed his laptop with a sigh. "Do you have your iPhone with you? I might as well get you hooked up now. Since you're not letting me get any work done."

"Sorry." I pulled a few blades of grass and threw them up in the air. They dropped in a clump on my lap.

The humidity seemed to stop everything from moving very far. Including me. "The iPhone's in my room."

"Bring it with you next time," Sonny said. "I'd like to take a look at it anyway."

"Guess you don't have one?"

Sonny shook his head. "Just this clunky old thing." He held up his laptop. It looked heavy. "I'd love to get an iPad, but Dad won't buy me one. And I can't pay for it myself because I can't get a job."

"Why not?"

"There aren't many jobs around here," Sonny replied, "and it's pretty hard to get into town."

"Living in the middle of nowhere must be bad," I said, "for so many reasons."

Sonny's jaw clenched. "There's nothing wrong with living in the country," he said slowly, with an edge to his voice.

"There doesn't seem to be anything too great about it either," I said without thinking.

"Not everyone wants to live in the city," Sonny said sharply, his voice suddenly louder, the words coming out more quickly.

I was stunned by his reaction. "I don't know, I just assumed…"

"Don't assume," Sonny said, cutting me off.

"So you like it here?"

"Of course I do."

"You're not anxious to get out?" I said, now choosing my words carefully. "Like Amber? She's always talking about moving to the city."

"Not exactly."

"What then?"

Sonny sighed again. "I want to go to the University of Guelph, get a degree in agriculture and be an organic farmer."

"You do?"

"Yes." Sonny said this quietly, without looking me in the eye.

"Well, then, you need to start by fighting for the land," I said.

"It's too late, Bree. That's what you don't seem to get. We don't farm the land anyway, and the highway is a done deal. There is no way to fight it."

I stared at Sonny. "You're just giving up?"

"I can farm somewhere else. Maybe join a co-op."

"You're giving up."

"I'm not giving up," Sonny said, "I'm accepting reality."

"Uncle Doug's still fighting," I said, feeling desperate.

"Dad's not fighting the highway so we can farm the land again. He's just trying to get as much out of it as he can." Sonny opened his computer and started pressing buttons to wake it up.

I stayed next to him, trying to figure out what to do with all this new information. "I fought a bylaw against tree climbing at Cedar Grove," I said, as much to myself as Sonny.

"Cedar Grove?" Sonny mumbled as he typed.

"My townhouse complex." Sonny didn't respond, so I added, "In Vancouver."

"I know where you live."

"Maybe I could tell you about it sometime. When you're not so busy."

"Maybe."

"There's some stuff on the Cedar Grove website, if you're interested," I said, ignoring the fact that he was very obviously not interested. "We won."

"I'm sure what you did was great," Sonny said, "but the highway is different." He looked up, straight at me this time. "There's nothing you can do."

"Maybe." I smiled and crossed my arms over my chest. "Maybe not."

I'd made up my mind. Doing nothing was not an option for me. Even if I didn't plan to be here for a minute longer than I had to be.

Chapter Six

Sonny connected my iPhone to their wireless the next day. I don't think it took him more than two minutes. I probably could have set it up myself if he'd just given me the password. But he really seemed to want to play around with it. Which he did. For hours.

When I finally got it back, I sat by the barn and called Sarah on Skype. I was missing her, missing home, and needed to talk to someone about the highway. Someone who understood me.

I told Sarah about Percy Murfin and the information meeting, and Uncle Doug saying that Grandma was insane, and about how he wanted to put her in a home. It took a while, because the picture kept freezing and my words sometimes got jumbled, but Sarah listened quietly as I blabbed on and on and on. When I was finally finished, she told me what I already knew. I had to talk to Percy Murfin.

"But I don't know how to get ahold of him," I told her.

"You'll figure it out," she replied.

"But how?" I moaned. And then, because part of me really didn't want it to be possible, I added, "It's impossible."

"Didn't you say there was an information notice or something? There must be a phone number on there somewhere. Just call and book an appointment." Sarah was always confident. She didn't get nervous about calling adults and booking appointments and making presentations. Not like I did.

"Yeah, I guess." A bigger part of me knew I would do whatever I had to do, no matter how nervous it made me.

As soon as Sarah and I were done talking, I went into the farmhouse to search for the meeting notice Percy Murfin had given me. I found it crumpled up in the corner of my room. Sure enough, there was a phone number listed on the bottom. Would that get me to Percy Murfin?

Without cell reception, I couldn't make the call on my iPhone, so I went to the kitchen and dialed the number on Grandma's old plug-in phone. My hands were shaking and I was trying to be quick in case Grandma came in from the garden. It took me three times to get the number right.

By the time the phone started ringing on the other end, my T-shirt was soaked with sweat. So anxious to get the conversation over with, I hadn't even thought about what I was going to say.

Not that it mattered. I didn't get to talk to Percy Murfin. But I did talk to a woman with a happy sing-song voice that made me feel a little less anxious. I quickly told her who I was and what I wanted. Without asking any questions, she very kindly made arrangements for Percy Murfin to come out to the farm on Monday morning at 10:30. I think she thought he was coming to meet with Grandma. Actually, I know she did, but I didn't correct the misunderstanding because I wasn't sure he would come if he knew he was only meeting with me. Grandma always volunteered at the hospital in Kitchener on Monday mornings. I plugged the date into the otherwise empty iCalender on my iPhone even though I knew I wouldn't forget.

I was happy to have done something about the highway and even happier that there was nothing else I could do for another four days. Four days was an eternity on the farm.

I started hanging out with Amber and Jasper more. I even spent some time with Sonny, who tolerated my presence without saying much. Before I knew it, Monday had arrived. It was like someone had over-wound the noisy clock in Grandma's living room, making time go faster. I felt totally unprepared when Grandma left for the hospital, leaving me sitting on the worn-out corduroy couch, watching dust dance in the sunlight that streamed through the unwashed living-room window.

I took out the notice and thought about calling to cancel my appointment with Percy Murfin. Instead, I took a deep breath, turned the notice over and smoothed out the wrinkles with my palm. On the back I wrote down the reasons I thought the highway should be stopped.

- *This land has been in my family for many, many years.*
- *Highway will split the land in half, and each half will be too small for farming.*

- *Sonny wants to be a farmer.*
- *Mr. Vandermeer, my social studies teacher, says that the world could run out of food if too much land is developed or used to grow biofuels.*
- *We have enough shopping malls and condos but not enough farms in Canada.*
- *Mr. Vandermeer also taught us about food security. Canadians need to grow more of our own food and import less.*
- *Grandma will not only lose her home, she'll be put in a home.*
- *Mrs. Kornitsky will have to put up with a lot of traffic noise.*
- *Roads are made for cars and trucks, which pollute the air and cause global warming.*
- *Expanding the GO Train is better than building new roads.*

I was still working on my list when the doorbell sounded its chimes, waking up the quiet farmhouse. I took another deep breath.

When I opened the door—gently so the knob wouldn't come off—Percy Murfin was standing there with his briefcase. He smiled. "Good Morning, Bree."

"Hi, P—uh, Mr. Murfin," I said.

"Can I come in?" Percy Murfin tilted his head, trying to look past me into the house. "I'm supposed to meet with your grandmother."

"Uh, sure," I said, moving aside so that Percy Murfin could step into the small front hallway. "But, uh, Grandma's not here right now."

"There must be some mistake." Percy Murfin opened his briefcase and pulled out his Blackberry. "My secretary told me we had an appointment."

"Well, actually, that was me," I said, staring down at Percy Murfin's polished shoes. They looked so important and businesslike next to my small bare feet. Why had I let Amber paint my toenails ten different colors? What was I doing?

"You wanted to meet with me?" The word *you* sounded so loud and deep coming from Percy Murfin that it made shudder. "About what?"

"The highway," I said quietly.

"Okay," Percy Murfin said with a loud sigh. "I've come all the way out here. Let's have a listen to what you have to say."

So we sat at the kitchen table. I went over my list, more or less. He didn't pull anything else out of his briefcase, and he didn't write anything down, but he did listen patiently. I liked him for that.

"That's it," I said when I couldn't think of anything else to say.

"That's pretty impressive," said Percy Murfin. "How old are you, Bree?"

"I'm turning twelve tomorrow," I said.

"Very impressive for a twelve-year-old," Percy Murfin said with a soft chuckle. "You are thinking of your family and your neighbors, and that's very sweet."

"Sweet?"

"But it's my job," Percy Murfin continued, "to think about the good of everyone. It's not just about one family."

"But I'm not just talking about my family—"

"This is just a small, rural stretch of land in the middle of an important transportation hub. Hundreds of thousands of people travel between Guelph and Kitchener every day. Even more travel from Kitchener and Guelph into Toronto for business. Not to mention trucks carrying goods. It's our job to keep the economy rolling." Percy Murfin laughed. "If you'll pardon the pun."

"But this land is special, Mr. Murfin."

"Why?"

"Well…"

"You're going to have to come up with something better than that if you want to stop the highway."

"Like what?"

Percy Murfin laughed again. "To be honest, Bree, nothing's going to stop this highway." He stood up. Under his breath he added, "Unless it's a Native burial ground or something."

"But—"

"Sorry, Bree," Percy Murfin interrupted, picking up his briefcase and striding toward the front door. "I'm going on holidays for a while, but please tell your grandmother that I'll return to finish up our negotiation as soon as I get back."

"Finish up?" I asked, trailing behind him.

"Yes, the highway construction is going to start in the fall. I'm going to need your grandmother to sign the papers by the end of August." He pulled open the door. The knob came off in his hand. With a shrug, he handed the knob over to me along with a business card he pulled out of his breast pocket. "Call me directly if you need anything else."

I took the card and the knob without saying a word.

"Good day, Bree," Percy Murfin said as he walked across the front porch.

I stood in the doorway and watched him step cautiously down the rickety stairs.

I knew I should thank him for coming. That would be the polite thing to do. But I wasn't feeling polite. Just the opposite. I was feeling frustrated. And totally helpless.

Chapter Seven

There was no big birthday greeting when I woke up on July 26. I don't even think Grandma said good morning when I came into the kitchen and poured no-name cereal into a chipped bowl, checking the date on the carton before adding milk.

But there was a card-sized envelope lying on the table next to my placemat with *Bree* written on the front in Grandma's favorite red ink. That made me feel good. I'd been trying to get Grandma to use my nickname since I'd arrived. Only teachers and doctors called me Brianna. And my mom—usually when I was in trouble.

When I was done eating, Grandma made me feel even better by asking what I wanted to do for my birthday. She thought we should go somewhere in town. Apparently Amber and Jasper wanted to come too.

Not knowing what there was to do in Kitchener, I said the first thing that came to mind. The library. I was thinking about the computer. Doing research on my iPhone was proving difficult. The signal by the barn was weak, and it was hard reading detailed stuff on the little screen.

Yesterday's frustration had turned into determination. If Percy Murfin needed a better reason to save the farm, I would find one. There had to be something about the land that made it too valuable to cover in asphalt. I remembered the time one of Mom's housing developments was stopped when a digger uncovered rocks that looked like arrowheads. Everything had been put on hold for months while archeologists sifted through the dirt for Native artifacts.

Grandma dropped us off at the library but didn't stay. Apparently she had a sick friend in town who could use a visit.

The library was okay, bigger than our local branch in Vancouver, but not as big as the Central Library downtown. We made ourselves comfortable.

Jasper played with puppets, and Amber flipped through fashion magazines while I checked my emails. My inbox was filled with birthday messages, which made me feel happy and sad at the same time.

When I was finally done with email, I started googling to see what I could find about the history of the farm. I didn't get very far. Probably because I didn't really know what I was looking for.

Before I was ready to leave the library, Grandma was back to pick us up, announcing that we were going to the Stockyards for lunch.

"Noooo," Amber said.

"Yes," Grandma said. "It's inexpensive and the food is decent."

"But it's Bree's birthday. Surely we can take her somewhere a little nicer. Somewhere without cows."

"We are going to the Stockyards," Grandma said firmly.

I didn't say a thing. I was starving and it didn't matter to me where we went. Anything would be better than the processed stuff I'd been eating at Grandma's, or the fussy dishes that Amber prepared. Not that I didn't appreciate their efforts. It's just that Dad's great cooking had spoiled me, I guess.

As it turned out, everything about the restaurant was the exact opposite of either processed or fussy. The Stockyards was actually the Ontario Livestock Exchange. The place where farmers come to buy and sell cows. The roast beef sandwich I ordered was delicious, with just the right amount of mustard, but it was hard to enjoy it with the smell of manure hanging so heavy in the air.

Our table was pretty quiet, so I watched the farmers as they walked in and out of the restaurant while we ate. There were a lot of them. And a lot of them seemed to know Grandma. She smiled and had something nice to say to each person who came by to say hello. At the end of the meal she ordered a coffee so we could stay a little longer.

Amber was busy sketching something on her napkin. Jasper was making a pyramid out of creamers. Grandma looked more relaxed and comfortable than she'd been since I arrived. I decided to try and make the most of it. "So, Grandma…" I started.

"What?"

"I was wondering…" I paused, trying to figure out what question might lead me to the information I wanted. "Do you know what the farmland was used for before the Bridges came along?"

"Your great-grandfather bought it from the government when he immigrated here from Germany."

"Was it already a farm?"

Grandma chuckled. "No, it was just bush. Your great-grandfather cleared the land. Grandpa was the one who farmed it. Started working when he was just a boy. Younger than you."

"Are you sure the land wasn't used for something before that?"

"That was a long time ago, Bree. There was a lot of unused land in Canada." Grandma took a sip of her coffee. "Why are you asking?"

"Jasper!" Amber suddenly hissed. "What are you doing down there?"

"Playing cave," Jasper said from under the table.

Amber put down her pencil. "Almost ready to go?" she asked Grandma.

"Almost," Grandma said, taking another sip of coffee.

"I'm just curious," I said, not wanting the conversation with Grandma to end even if it didn't seem to be getting me anywhere. "Something interesting must have happened on the farm before we came along."

"Nothing interesting ever happens around here," Amber interjected, "and I'm sure it never did."

"There must be something," I said. "Maybe from the days of cowboys and Indians?"

"Why so many questions?" Grandma pushed away her empty coffee cup. "Did you find something?"

A familiar voice interrupted us. "Hello, Bridges family!" I looked up to see Mrs. Kornitsky approaching our table.

"Holly," Grandma said.

"Hello, Mrs. Kornitsky," Amber said. "Look, Jasper, it's Mrs. Kornitsky."

"Hi, Mrs. Corn," mumbled a voice from under the table.

Mrs. Kornitsky put her arm on my shoulder. "Be careful, Bree. Your face will stay like that if the wind changes." I hadn't realized I was frowning.

"You've met?" asked Grandma.

I smiled at Mrs. Kornitsky and nodded.

"My granddaughters are complaining that nothing ever happens on the farm," Grandma explained.

"Oh, we've had our fair share of excitement," said Mrs. Kornitsky. "Seen a lot of change, and now we've got this highway to deal with."

I could sense Grandma's mood change as soon as Mrs. Kornitsky said the word *highway*. I jumped in, trying to steer the conversation. "Got any good stories for us? From the olden days?"

Mrs. Kornitsky sat down in Jasper's empty seat. "Well, there was the time that reporter from *The Record* came around asking questions about an old cemetery on our property."

Mrs. Kornitsky and Grandma both laughed. Then Grandma said, "That was only a couple of years ago."

"What happened?" I asked.

"Oh, nothing. The reporter had fallen hook, line and sinker for some tall tale about a convict cemetery," Mrs. Kornitsky said. "There were some interesting rumors flying around about it for a while, but nothing ever came of it."

"Can we go now?" Amber asked. "I think Jasper's had enough."

"But Mrs. Kornitsky just got here," I objected, unable to hide the fact that Amber's interruptions were starting to annoy me.

"I should be on my way. I'm meeting my sister for a cup of tea," Mrs. Kornitsky said as she lifted the tablecloth and bent over to look under the table. "See you later, Jasper."

"Bye, Mrs. Corn."

"Remember my invitation," said Mrs. Kornitsky, looking at me with raised eyebrows. "Milk and cookies."

"Thanks," I said, and then added my voice to the chorus of goodbyes from Grandma and Amber.

When Mrs. Kornitsky was gone, Amber turned to me and said, "For your birthday." She handed me a beautifully wrapped box.

"For me?" I took the package, feeling more than a little guilty for being annoyed at Amber. "Thanks."

"Open it," Amber said.

I did. Inside was a skirt made of at least five different fabrics, each with its own texture and shade of blue. When I held it up, I could see that the layers of fabric hung together like waves. The ocean effect was highlighted by a silver pattern that flowed from one layer of fabric into another. I'd never seen anything like it before.

"It's awesome," I said. "Where'd you get it?"

"I made it," Amber said with a small smile.

"For real?"

"Yes. For real."

"Amber's very talented," Grandma said.

"No kidding," I took a closer look at the skirt. "This is amazing."

"Glad you like it," Amber said, her cheeks turning pink. "I designed it just for you."

"Thank you," I said again. I didn't know what else to say. My birthday had certainly turned out a lot better than I'd thought it would.

"Let's go home," Grandma said, grabbing the check.

Home. The farm still didn't feel like home, but it was definitely starting to feel a little less strange. At least this hadn't been the worst birthday ever.

Chapter Eight

Mrs. Kornitsky hadn't given me a lot, but she'd given me enough. A Google search using the words *Breslau convict cemetery* led me right to an article in *The Record*. In it was an interview with a retired RCMP officer who remembered being taken to a graveyard in the bush. A graveyard for criminals who'd been hanged in the early 1900s.

It seemed like the reporter had tried to dig up additional information. She'd done interviews and researched the archives, but she hadn't had much luck. Instead, she'd filled the article with facts about the history of the death penalty in Canada. There was a simple map next to the article. It made more sense than the survey maps I'd seen at the highway meeting, but it still wasn't super clear, because I didn't recognize all the landmarks.

I climbed up Gnarly and tried to figure it out. From the top of the tree I could see the corn fields, the soy fields, the barn and the two houses. There was something comforting about their organization. Long, straight lines created rectangles of different sizes that covered most of the property. From this distance, you couldn't tell that Grandma's house was falling apart or that the barn was full of rusty, old industrial stoves and fridges. The buildings looked over the fields as if they were in command. Like they were a part of the land, not something that had been built on it.

None of this was on the map.

My view from the top of Gnarly included the road at the end of the long lane, congested with cars even though it was early afternoon. Nowhere close to rush hour. The road was on the map, of course. It had probably been a horse track back when the land was being used as a cemetery. Soon to be replaced by a super-highway, unless I could do something to stop it.

Also on the map was a creek that looked like it ran diagonally across one corner of the land. I couldn't see a creek from Gnarly, just an area of bush where I guessed it might be.

Only one thing was obvious. If I was going to uncover anything the reporter had missed, I needed the help of someone who knew the farm well. Really well. Someone like Sonny.

It took me a while to track him down. When I found him, he was in one of the fields behind the barn.

"What are you doing?" I called out to him as I pushed through the corn rows, which no longer seemed as logical and orderly as they had from the top of the tree.

"Nothing," Sonny mumbled in reply.

"Come on," I said, out of breath now that I was finally standing next to him. "You're obviously doing something."

Sonny was hunched over, holding something that looked like the test tubes we used in science lab. "Taking samples," he said.

"Samples of what?"

"Soil."

"Why?"

"Because."

"Because why?" I was trying not to sound annoyed. I wanted Sonny to help me. I didn't want him to get mad at me. That would be bad.

"Because I'm interested." Sonny stood up and put the glass tube in his backpack. There was a clinking sound of glass against glass as he zipped up the pack.

"Are you done?" I asked.

He strapped on his pack. "For now," he replied.

"Good," I said with a big smile, "then maybe you can help me out with something?"

"Something like what?" Sonny was already walking away from me. Down the row in the direction I'd just come from.

I followed him. "I need help finding a convict cemetery."

He stopped abruptly and turned to face me. "Finding what?"

"A convict cemetery."

"Tell me more."

I told him about the conversation with Mrs. Kornitsky, the article in *The Record* and the map.

"That's kinda cool," he said when I was done, "but I don't understand what it has to do with the highway."

"Mr. Murfin says we can save the land if we find a good enough reason."

"But a convict cemetery? Who's going to want to save that? You need a Native hunting ground or an endangered animal."

"Endangered animal?"

"Yeah. Like the spotted owl."

"There are spotted owls here?"

"No, that was somewhere in BC. Vancouver Island, I think. Where they stopped the clearcutting of an old-growth forest because the land was home to a family of northern spotted owls that were facing extinction."

"They did?" My brain was searching through Mr. Vandermeer's social studies lessons about old-growth logging.

"Shouldn't you know this stuff? You live in BC *and* you're an activist."

Me? An activist? I didn't know whether to be flattered or angry. I liked the idea of being an activist. But Sonny had a way of making me feel really dumb.

"Anyway, I'm sure there are other examples," Sonny said as he made his way out of the corn field. "But a convict cemetery?"

"That's all I've got," I said, trailing behind him again. "Will you help me or not?"

Sonny hesitated, and then he said, "Sure, why not?"

When we were out of the field, I handed my iPhone to Sonny so he could look at the map I had downloaded from the newspaper article. "Do you know where it is?"

"I think so," Sonny said, digging through his pack. "It's a good thing I brought these." He pulled out a pair of heavy-duty pruners, which turned out to be very useful as we bushwhacked our way through the back end of the property.

"I still don't think this is going to save the farm," Sonny said as we crawled through the dirt on our hands and knees.

I rolled my eyes, not wanting to deal with Sonny's doubts. "They can't build a highway over an important historical landmark," I said.

"They were criminals," Sonny said. "Guys who did something horrible enough to get hung for their crimes."

I didn't say anything else. I was grateful for Sonny's help and glad he didn't mind digging around in the dirt. He was certainly enjoying it more than I was. I'd choose climbing in the trees over crawling on the ground any day.

I got discouraged pretty quick. The whole thing was turning out to be a lot harder than I'd thought it would be. I'm not sure what I expected. A sign pointing me in the direction of some gravestones?

"Maybe we should give up," I said after a while. "At least for today."

"Just a few more minutes," Sonny said. "I think I might have found something."

My heart jumped with excitement but fell just as fast as I looked around. There was nothing here but overgrown blackberry bushes. "Come on, Sonny," I said. "I'm hungry. And the bugs are starting to come out."

"But there's evidence of an old trail here," Sonny said, walking ahead.

I couldn't see evidence of anything, but I followed him anyway. After all, this whole thing had been my idea.

"Here," Sonny said.

"What?" I said, catching up to him.

Sonny moved aside so I could see. "A clearing," he said.

Sonny's imaginary path had led us to the edge of the bush. Beyond it were two rows of widely spaced trees. "So?"

"That stream over there is the boundary between our property and Mrs. Kornitsky's." Sonny pointed toward a trickle of water that seemed to come from nowhere. "According to the map, the gravesite is within this old maple grove."

I whistled softly, totally impressed with Sonny. "What do we do now?" I asked.

"We search the area. You start here and I'll start over there at the other end," Sonny said.

I had no idea what I was looking for. "Okay," I said, hoping I would know it when I saw it.

As Sonny walked away, I looked up at the trees. They were nothing like the wide, moss-covered trees that filled the forests around Vancouver. These trees were tall and straight, with smooth, dry bark. Some of them looked pretty good for climbing. The bigger ones anyway. I circled one, wondering if I could find my way back to this spot on my own. I was so sure we weren't going to find evidence of a gravesite that I'd already starting thinking of plan B. Maybe there was a spotted owl or some other endangered bird roosting in these trees.

Suddenly, the ground under my foot dipped. "Ouch," I yelled as my ankle rolled over. With a thud, I landed on my butt.

Sonny came running. "You okay?" he asked.

"I think I twisted my ankle," I said, holding my foot up for him to see.

Sonny was on the ground next to me, but he wasn't paying any attention to me or my ankle.

"I'm not sure I can walk," I said, even though I was pretty sure I could.

"Uh-huh," Sonny said as he got up and started moving the dirt around with his foot.

"Thanks for caring," I muttered under my breath.

After a minute, Sonny stopped. "I think you found it Bree," he said.

"What?"

"The grave," he said. "There's one here."

"Where?"

"You're lying in a sunken pit," Sonny said, pointing out the indentation in the ground.

"What?" I got up quickly, forgetting all about my ankle.

"It's the size of a coffin," Sonny said.

A shiver ran down my spine as I stepped out of the shallow hole. I looked around. There were lots of pits. All the same size.

We stood there in silence. I rubbed by arms, which were covered with goose bumps. I was freezing, despite the heat.

"So this is it," I said at last. "The Breslau Convict Cemetery."

Chapter Nine

"Aren't you creeped out?" Sonny asked. "Amber would be so creeped out by the idea of dead bodies."

I wrapped my arms around my waist and tried to sound brave. "I'm just excited we found the gravesite. And I'm pretty sure the bodies aren't here anymore."

"You think the bodies have been moved?"

"That's what it said in the newspaper article. They must have been dug up before the province sold the land for farming."

"Why would anyone care about this site if the bodies aren't even here?"

I shrugged. "They might be here. They might not. It's still an important place."

I started taking pictures with my iPhone. I took quite a few. The graves were pretty obvious, now that I knew they were there, but I wasn't sure they would look like much in a photo.

"What are you going to do now?" Sonny asked. "Now that you have physical evidence of the cemetery. The evidence you wanted."

"Talk to Mr. Murfin again."

"He's not going to care," Sonny said.

"Then I'll take these photos to *The Record*," I said. "People have the right to know that this highway will be covering up an important part of our history."

"You really think people are going to care about some old cemetery for criminals?"

I nodded. "Maybe we've got a way of fighting the highway now."

If only it had been that easy.

I called the number on Percy Murfin's card right away, before I had time to get nervous. It wasn't until I got his voice mail that I remembered what he'd said about going on holiday. According to the message, he wasn't coming back for another two weeks.

Two weeks was too long. It was already August, and I was leaving at the end of the month. If I was going to do something with this graveyard information, I had to do it fast.

I went back to the article in *The Record* to find the name of the reporter. Jennifer Sharp. I tried contacting her through the newspaper website by sending an email. The message I got back didn't get me very far. Apparently, she worked there only as a freelance reporter. And they weren't allowed to give out contact information on their freelance reporters. Whatever that meant.

I wasn't sure what else to do so I went back to the convict cemetery. Not to see the gravesites. More to prove that I could find my way back. On my own. And also to climb a couple of trees.

When I got near the top of a tree I'd named Skeleton because it didn't have any leaves, I caught a glimpse of a house on the neighboring property. I assumed it belonged to Mrs. Kornitsky and decided it was time to take her up on the invitation for milk and cookies. Maybe the cookies would be homemade. And maybe I could get some more information.

Making my way through the overgrown maple grove onto Mrs. Kornitsky's property was easy. The cemetery was much closer to her farmhouse than ours. And there was no bush hugging the edge of her farm fields, which were filled with soybeans and corn, just like ours.

Mrs. Kornitsky was happy to see me. And the cookies were homemade. Chocolate chip.

"Looks as though you're enjoying your time in the country, Bree," said Mrs. Kornitsky, surveying the mud on my running shoes and the scratches on my arms and legs from bushwhacking.

"More than I thought I would," I replied honestly. It's not something I would have admitted to my family.

"You were asking about the history of the farm the other day. Did you get any stories out of your grandma?"

"No. She won't say much about the farm. Or the highway. Or anything, really."

Mrs. Kornitsky nodded. "She's been like that since your grandpa passed away. We used to be the best of friends. Still are, I suppose, but it's not the same."

Silence settled between us as I thought about Grandpa. It never really occurred to me how much she must miss him.

Mrs. Kornitsky offered me another cookie. "If there's anything you need to know, you can always ask me."

"You've already helped a lot," I replied. Then I told her what Sonny and I had found.

"Well, I'll be darned. You mean there's actually something there?"

"You can see the spaces in the ground where the graves used to be," I said.

"That reporter would've been pleased as punch to find those."

"I was thinking she might still be interested."

"Oh, I'm not so sure," Mrs. Kornitsky said. "That was a while back. Things don't stay news-worthy for long."

"But don't you think the information is even more important now? Now that they're planning to pave over it?"

"Maybe," Mrs. Kornitsky said slowly. "Maybe."

"I called the newspaper," I told her.

"You did?"

"Yes, but they wouldn't put me in touch with the reporter."

"How very grown-up of you, Bree." Mrs. Kornitsky said as she started shifting through the piles of paper on her kitchen table.

"I guess." I looked at the mess. The piles covered the table and the bookshelf behind it. Envelopes, magazines, information flyers. It didn't look like Mrs. Kornitsky ever threw anything away. "What is all this stuff?"

"I spend a lot of time writing letters and collecting things that may be of interest to my friends," Mrs. Kornitsky explained. "I have pen pals all over the world."

"Oh," I said.

After she'd moved everything around, Mrs. Kornitsky announced, "It's not here. Too old. I'll be right back."

While she was gone, I glanced through the papers now scattered next to my empty plate. One with the word *PETITION* at the top in bold letters grabbed my attention, but I didn't have time to examine it before Mrs. Kornitsky came back into the kitchen.

"This is going to knock your socks off, Bree," she said.

"What?"

"I found it."

"Found what?"

"Phone number and"—Mrs. Kornitsky squinted at the small scrap of paper in her hand—"an email address maybe?" She handed me the paper. "For the reporter. Jennifer Sharp."

I smiled. "You think I should call her?"

"Would I dig up the phone number if I didn't think you should call her?" Mrs. Kornitsky handed me a phone receiver that reminded me of one I'd seen in a scary old movie. I looked down at the coils of the long black cord stretching across the kitchen table.

"Now?" I was suddenly feeling nervous. The whole thing didn't seem so easy anymore. What if the reporter didn't remember the original story? What if she didn't care? What if she didn't want to help? That would be bad.

"This is no time for cold feet," Mrs. Kornitsky said. She was already dialing.

"Maybe I should send an email." I needed more time to think. More time to prepare. So I didn't blow the chance. Our last chance to save the farm.

"Hooey," Mrs. Kornitsky said, now practically holding the receiver to my ear.

I took a deep breath. It didn't help.

As it turned out, I was right to be nervous.

Chapter Ten

The phone rang two times before she answered. "Jennifer Sharp."

"Uh, can I speak to Jennifer Sharp?" I asked, feeling dumb the minute the words were out of my mouth.

"Speaking."

"Oh," I replied. "Hello, Ms. Sharp."

"Who is this?"

"Um…" I took another deep breath. "My name is Brianna Bridges, and I live, well, my grandma lives on a farm in Breslau and you did a story about it a little while ago for *The Record*?" All of this came tumbling out so fast I didn't have a chance to breathe again until I was done.

"I did a story about a farm?" Jennifer Sharp asked.

"Not exactly about the farm," I said, trying to slow myself down. "It was actually about an old gravesite for convicts."

"My story on the history of capital punishment in Ontario?"

"I guess," I said, hoping we were talking about the same thing. I looked up at Mrs. Kornitsky. She was nodding so much she looked like one of those bobble-head dolls. I was glad she was there next to me.

"What about it?" Jennifer Sharp asked.

"Well, I've got some new information. I thought you might be interested," I said.

"Go on," said Jennifer Sharp. Her voice had gone from direct but polite to abrupt and impatient.

"My cousin Sonny and I found the cemetery."

"And?"

"There are actually gravesites there. You can still see the evidence."

"So?"

"So I thought you might be interested in doing another story. Now that there's something to prove you were right."

"Right about what?"

"Right about the gravesite. Right that it exists."

"There was never any doubt about the gravesite. All the information is in the archives."

"But you were here," I insisted, "asking questions. Trying to find evidence."

"I don't really remember that," Jennifer Sharp said. "I was probably looking for a story angle."

"Story angle?"

I heard Jennifer Sharp let out a deep breath. "Listen, I have to go. I'm on a deadline. Is there something else I can help you with?"

"No," I said slowly, "I guess not."

There was silence on the other end of the phone. Not the reaction I wanted. "It's just that the highway…" I said, desperately hoping she hadn't already hung up.

"What about the highway?"

"The new highway they're building will go right over the old cemetery."

"Highway Seven?"

"Yes."

"Does that mean the highway will go through your grandma's farm?"

"Yes."

"What did you say your name was again?"

"Brianna Bridges."

"How old are you?"

"Eleven," I said quickly. Too quickly. "Twelve, actually."

"Is there a way I can contact you? Or maybe I could come out to the farm to see you sometime?"

"I guess," I said, feeling confused. I gave her my email address and directions to the farm. Then I asked, "Does this mean you're interested in doing another story about the cemetery?"

"The cemetery? No, I don't care about the cemetery."

"Oh," I said.

"But I might be in touch about another story," Jennifer Sharp continued, "if that's okay."

"I guess," I said, too overwhelmed to ask any more questions.

"Thanks for calling," Jennifer said.

Before I could say another word, she hung up.

I handed the phone back to Mrs. Kornitsky. "How'd it go?" she asked.

"I don't know," I said, feeling the sting of tears behind my eyes. "She doesn't care about the gravesite at all."

"Well, at least you tried," Mrs. Kornitsky said.

"Trying isn't good enough."

"Have another cookie."

"No, thanks," I said looking down at my plate so Mrs. Kornitsky wouldn't see the tears that were threatening to spill. That's when I noticed the petition still lying there between the crumbs and my empty milk glass. I picked it up. "What's this?"

"What?" Mrs. Kornitsky asked as she pulled her reading glasses down from their perch on the top of her head.

"This," I said, handing it to her.

"Oh that. It's my petition for concrete driveway surfaces."

"Driveway surfaces?"

"Yes. When the highway goes in, they're going to replace our driveways. They're planning to put in gravel 'cause that's what we have now. But I want concrete," Mrs. Kornitsky explained.

"Are you serious?"

"Serious as a snail," Mrs. Kornitsky said with a laugh. "A lot of my neighbors want concrete too."

I looked at the list of names, signatures and addresses. My body filled with heat, drying my eyes and leaving me hot with anger.

Why was Mrs. Kornitsky trying to get a better driveway? Shouldn't she be fighting to stop the highway?

Why was I the only one who cared?

Chapter Eleven

I did my best to avoid Mrs. Kornitsky after that. And Grandma. Even Sonny. All the people who said they didn't want the highway but refused to do anything about it. I was tired of being angry.

At first I spent a lot of time in my room. But that got really boring really quick. There was nothing to do except read. And reading is not really my thing.

When Sonny wasn't around, I hung out by the barn using my iPhone to communicate with Sarah and Michael. Not trying to get any advice, just trying to concentrate on Cedar Grove and my friends there. I was going home soon. And I was done caring about what was going to happen to the farm after I was gone.

The only people I really spent any time with were Amber and Jasper. I got into a bit of a routine of going over there in the afternoon to play with Jasper while Amber sketched or sewed or dyed fabric or whatever. Being an aspiring clothing designer seemed to keep her really busy.

Sometimes Amber would ask me to be her model and I would sit there as still as I could, hoping not to get pricked with a pin, while she asked me questions about Vancouver. She couldn't get enough of my stories about Cedar Grove, about living so close to so many other kids my age.

Amber didn't have many friends, for lots of different reasons. Her school was small, for starters, even though they bused kids in from far away. And none of her classmates had the same interests as Amber. The few girls she did get along with lived too far away for a short visit, which was all Amber had time for because of Jasper. She didn't sound sorry for herself as she explained all this. For her, it just seemed to be a fact of life.

None of it seemed fair to me. My dad would never let me miss out on time with my friends. And although he gave me chores to do, he always insisted that my number one job was being a kid. Uncle Doug was so different from my dad, it was hard to believe they were brothers. I didn't understand why he expected Amber to do so much.

Taking care of Jasper sure seemed like a lot of responsibility. In September, he'd be going into all-day kindergarten, but she'd been looking after him every summer since Aunt Theresa died. As Amber and I got to know each other better, I started staying for dinner more often. Grandma joined us when she didn't have a sick or lonely friend to visit. Sonny usually showed up just in time to eat, but he always disappeared into his room as soon as the meal was done.

Uncle Doug was almost never there. I assumed he came home after I left. And I only ever hung around long enough to help clean up. Avoiding him was easy.

But one day he surprised me. Surprised us all, actually. Including Amber, who'd made wild mushroom risotto for dinner. Not Uncle Doug's favorite. Surprise, surprise.

I was doing the dishes when Uncle Doug came up and asked if we could talk. Amber was helping Jasper get ready for bed. Grandma had already gone home.

"I guess," I said, handing him a kitchen towel. If I was going to be stuck in the kitchen with him, he might was well help out. It was really starting to bug me that Amber did all the work around here.

Uncle Doug took the towel. "I understand you had a talk with Mr. Murfin," he said.

"Where'd you hear that?" I asked. I could feel my heart start to beat a little faster.

"He told me," Uncle Doug replied.

"He's back?" I asked, wondering how two weeks had gone by so quickly.

"I met with him this morning."

"Oh."

"I don't appreciate you interfering, Brianna."

I turned back to the sink and plunged my hands into the warm soapy water, wishing I could jump right in and disappear. "What do you mean?"

"I'm negotiating with Mr. Murfin," said Uncle Doug, "trying to look after the best interests of the farm and everyone involved. I don't need your help."

I spun around as if Uncle Doug had pulled my hair. The anger I'd been trying so hard to contain suddenly came spilling out of me. "You don't care about the best interests of the farm or anyone who lives here! You just want to ship Grandma off to some loony-bin old-folks home and turn this land into a mall. All you care about is money."

Uncle Doug put down the dish towel. He hadn't dried a single thing. "Is that what Sonny told you?"

I nodded, too angry to open my mouth again. I felt like I had no control over what might come out.

"Figures," Uncle Doug said, crossing his arms.

"It's not true?" I asked through clenched teeth.

"Let's just say that Sonny and I don't exactly see eye to eye on this."

"What's that supposed to mean?"

"We've had this argument before," Uncle Doug replied.

"You have?"

"Many times. This highway business has been going on for a long time. There's been lots of consultation. Lots of opportunities for the people living around here to tell the province what they think."

"Then why have you let it happen? Why are you letting them turn the land into a highway?"

"I'm not *letting* them do anything. The highway was always going to happen whether we like it or not. I'm just trying to make the most of it."

I put my wet hands on my hips. "Get rich from it, you mean."

Uncle Doug sighed. "I'm going to tell you what I keep telling Sonny. This land has no value as a farm. If we sell it all to the government we make one small sum of money and that's it. But if we keep a bit of the land, we can capitalize on the opportunity and make a killing. Enough to support this family for many, many years."

"But what about Sonny's dream of becoming a farmer? And what about Grandma?"

"This isn't going to stop Sonny from being a farmer. Not if that's what he really wants to do."

"And Grandma?" I repeated. "This is her home!"

"It'll be hard on your grandma. We'll figure out what's best for her when the time comes. She'll be okay. Trust me."

I stared at Uncle Doug, not sure what to say. I'd heard him call Grandma crazy! And now I was supposed to trust him to do what's best for her?

"Grandma will be okay," Uncle Doug said again.

"But she's so unhappy!" I blurted out.

Uncle Doug gave a slight nod with his chin. It was such a small movement I hardly even noticed. Then he said, "She's unhappy all right."

"How can you not want to make it better for her?"

"I do. I wish I could." Uncle Doug hesitated. "If only it were that simple."

"But we could stop the highway," I insisted, "instead of just trying to profit from it."

"Even if stopping the highway was possible, it wouldn't be enough to make Grandma happy." Uncle Doug stopped and examined his fingers. "Grandma's unhappiness goes a lot deeper than that."

"It does?"

Uncle Doug nodded again, more forcefully this time. "Anyway, Bree, I'd appreciate if you could keep quiet about this highway business. Until I've finished my negotiations with Mr. Murfin."

"According to Mr. Murfin, there's nothing to negotiate."

"We'll see about that," Uncle Doug said, his arms now hanging weakly at his sides, as if in defeat.

I turned back to the sink without saying a word.

After a minute I heard the floor creak as Uncle Doug walked away. "Thanks, Bree," he said as he left the room. "Thanks for keeping quiet."

Thanks?

Uncle Doug obviously didn't know me well enough to realize that keeping quiet is not my thing.

Chapter Twelve

Now I needed to stop the highway *and* find out why Grandma was so unhappy. The question was—which would be harder?

At the Stockyards on my birthday, Grandma had asked whether I'd found anything. I figured that meant there was something to find. So I started looking. I waited until she was volunteering at the hospital or out doing her weekly errands. Then I wandered through the farmhouse like I was playing hide-and-seek with Grandma's unhappiness.

The farmhouse wasn't much bigger than our townhouse in Vancouver. Instead of seven small rooms spread over three levels, like in Cedar Grove, there were five big rooms all on the same floor. The basement didn't count because I'd never go down there. It was dark and damp and smelled like cooked cabbage from the days when Grandma made sauerkraut.

The farmhouse had three bedrooms. I was sleeping in the one that used to belong to Dad. It looked like a cross between a nine-year-old boy's room and a hockey shrine. Dusty trophies filled the bookshelf. Banners and pennants covered the walls. There was even paraphernalia from Dad's days with the Sheffield Steelers, his hockey team in England, where he played long after he'd moved away from the farm.

I was tempted to go into Grandma's bedroom. If there was something to find, it was sure to be in there. But I couldn't even open the door. As much as I wanted answers, I didn't want to invade her privacy. That would be bad.

The third bedroom was Uncle Doug's old room, although it didn't look like it had ever belonged to a teenager. It looked more like a scrapyard. Or a used bookstore. The double bed in the middle of the room had been stripped of sheets and pillows. Stacked on top of the bare mattress was more junk than I'd ever seen: old toys, boxes of clothes, broken clocks, sporting equipment, even a record player.

I made a small space on the bed so I could sit and look at the bookshelf, which was also full to overflowing. I had to look through a lot of Uncle Doug's old school work before I finally found something interesting. As I pulled out the buried photo album, a pile of pictures fell into my lap. There was Grandpa, perched on top of the tractor, a huge smile plastered on his face as he squinted into the sun.

I was looking through the rest of the pictures when I sensed movement behind me. Turning quickly, I found Grandma standing in the doorway.

"Grandma!" I put the photo album down. "I didn't hear you come in."

"What are you doing in here?"

"Just looking at pictures," I answered. "I didn't know I wasn't allowed."

"You're allowed. Of course, you're allowed. I've nothing to hide."

"Okay, then…" I started to reply but Grandma was already gone.

I turned back to the bookshelf and pulled out another album. I flipped through more pictures but didn't find anything good. Just some scenery shots and a bunch of photos of people I didn't recognize.

As I was looking through some out-of-focus animal pictures, presumably from a family trip to the zoo, Grandma returned. She came right into the room this time, wading through the junk on the floor, and started moving stuff around without saying a word. Picking up an old pair of skates, she cleared a spot next to me on the bed. When she sat down, our shoulders were touching.

Grandma still hadn't said anything so I held up a picture of Uncle Doug carrying Dad on his shoulders. Grandpa appeared to be chasing them. They were playing in front of a barn so red I almost didn't recognize it. "This is my favorite," I said.

She took it from me and stared at it for a long time. "So many memories," she finally said.

I should have kept quiet. Let Grandma talk. But I felt uncomfortable. I was worried she might cry. That would be bad. So instead I asked, "How was your day?"

Then I listened patiently as Grandma told me about the time she'd spent at the hospital that morning. Turns out she's a volunteer grandparent at the neonatal intensive care unit. Which basically means she spent hours cuddling premature babies when their parents weren't around.

"Why do you volunteer there?" I asked without thinking. This wasn't the talking I wanted Grandma to do, but I was curious. I didn't understand why she spent so much time helping strangers when her own grandchildren could use some help.

"Those babies need me."

"Oh."

"I like to be needed," Grandma continued, "and I'm not really needed here anymore." Grandma looked at the picture she was still holding in her hand. "Not like I was back then."

I didn't understand, but I was happy Grandma was talking, so I blurted out the question I really wanted to ask. "What are you going to do once the farm is sold?"

"Oh, I don't know," Grandma said, looking away. "I try not to think about it."

"But don't you think you should?"

"Why are you so worried about it, Bree?"

"Because it's going to happen really soon. I think you should be prepared."

"Prepared? To lose my home? Impossible." Grandma put down the picture and placed her hands on the bed like she was getting ready to stand.

"Wait," I said, not wanting the conversation to end. Grandma frowned. "What?"

"Do you know that Uncle Doug wants to put you in a home?"

Grandma's frown deepened, exaggerating the wrinkles on her face. She slouched forward, looking defeated. Like she'd just finished a marathon. In last place.

I picked at my fingernails while I waited for her to respond. "I figured," she said quietly. So quietly that I felt it through our connected shoulders more clearly than I heard it.

"Is that what you want?"

I watched Grandma as she ran her fingers along the jumbled row of photo albums still on the shelf. "No," she said.

"Then why don't you do something about it?"

"I've already told you, Bree, there is no way to fight this highway. Or your Uncle Doug. It's going to happen whether I like it or not."

"If that's true," I said slowly, "then don't you think you should figure out what you're going to do when it happens?"

"I don't want to live anywhere else."

"But you have to live somewhere."

"I'll just go where they tell me to go."

"But Uncle Doug wants to put you in a home," I said. "A home for *old* people. You're too young for that!"

The wrinkles on Grandma's face smoothed a little as she laughed softly. "I'm not young, Bree."

"You're healthy, and…" I hesitated, searching for a word that meant the opposite of crazy. "Healthy and smart. You volunteer and help people and…stuff."

"I'm also tired. I don't eat very well, and I don't feel like cleaning up anymore. I haven't been able to take care of this place for years. Maybe it's time. Time for someone to take care of me."

"But an old-folks home? That's for people who need help going to the bathroom!" I'd visited my other gran in one of those places. Only once, because she lived in England. But I remembered it clearly, with its dark halls and smelly rooms.

Grandma was quiet. She was no longer frowning. But she wasn't smiling either. She was just staring out into space. Like her eyes had gone blank.

"There has to be something besides an old-folks home," I insisted.

"Like what?" Grandma exclaimed, suddenly coming back to life. "One of those cheap houses they're building in Riverland? I might as well live in a cardboard box on the side of the road."

"Riverland?"

Grandma sighed. "It's a new community they're developing along the Grand River just outside of Breslau."

"What about a condo? I noticed they were building some near the Stockyards when we went to Kitchener for my birthday."

Grandma snorted. "A condominium? Surrounded by concrete? That's not for me. I need my garden. I need my space."

"Some of them are pretty big. The ones in Vancouver anyway. And some of them have gardens. One of my mom's friends lives on the ground floor of a ten-story condo building in False Creek. She has a huge garden." I said this really fast, so Grandma couldn't interrupt.

"A garden in a condo? Does she grow anything?"

"Yes, veggies and everything. She even has a fig tree," I responded, still talking fast. "And the best thing is that you don't have to cut the grass or shovel the snow, and there is less space to clean. Plus, you get to live next to people like you and make friends. I love living in Cedar Grove!"

"You do?"

"Of course," I said, surprised that Grandma would think otherwise. "Our townhouse is awesome."

"I always thought you lived there because your parents couldn't afford a house. Vancouver is so expensive."

"Well, yeah, I guess, but I don't think houses are so great. Sarah's mom's house in Surrey is big and messy and full of stuff. And they always have to stay home on the weekend to work on the house and garden."

Grandma was staring at me. "I see."

"So you'd consider it? A condo, I mean? Because that would be so much better for you than an old-folks home. You'd still have your own kitchen and your own room, and you wouldn't be surrounded by all those old people."

"For now I'm staying here," Grandma said, getting up from the bed. "I plan to enjoy the farmhouse for as long as I can. This highway will be built. Eventually. But it's not being built today."

"Not today, but soon. According to Percy Murfin anyway."

"Maybe, maybe not. There's been plenty of delays. I'm not going to waste my energy worrying about it."

"But…"

"No more, Bree." Grandma was already walking out the bedroom door. "I'm going to heat up some soup. You hungry?"

"Be there in a minute," I said. But Grandma was already gone. Leaving me alone with her memories.

Chapter Thirteen

Things seemed brighter in the farmhouse after that. Grandma and I spent some time together in the garden. We started talking more. That's how I found out Percy Murfin was coming to meet with her on Friday. He finally had something for her to sign.

I hadn't told Percy Murfin about the convict cemetery. And I hadn't found endangered birds in any of the trees I'd climbed. Not that I thought either of them would stop the highway. Not anymore.

I needed another plan, and I needed it right away. I was going home in two days. I had to show Percy Murfin I wasn't the only one who wanted to stop the highway.

So I started a petition.

I borrowed Sonny's bike. Without asking. I'd never seen him ride it, so I didn't think he'd notice it was gone. And I didn't want to answer a whole bunch of questions about why I needed it. I knew he'd try to stop me. That would be bad.

Halfway down the lane, I started questioning the whole petition thing myself. I wasn't even off the farm and already I was covered with dust. The road was bumpy and rough. And the bike's chain was in desperate need of some oil. Or something.

It was going to take forever to collect signatures out here in the country. But I didn't know what else to do. So I pushed forward, wishing this was Cedar Grove, where I could fill a page with signatures just by walking down the street.

Nobody answered the door at the first house. Or the second.

At the third house, I thought I'd hit the jackpot. I was wrong.

"Hi there," I said to the well-dressed woman who opened the door. She reminded me of Ethan's mom, Ms. Matheson, who was always wearing business suits and uncomfortable-looking shoes.

"What do you want?" the woman asked. She sounded a bit like Ethan's mom too.

I took a deep breath and imagined myself talking to Ms. Matheson. It helped to calm me down. A little. Ms. Matheson used to make me nervous, but not so much anymore. Not since I got her to listen to me about Cedar Grove's tree-climbing bylaw.

"I was wondering if you would be interested in signing this petition." I held up the lined piece of paper I'd made into a chart like the one I'd seen at Mrs. Kornitsky's. *Name. Address. Signature.*

The woman stared right at me, not even glancing at the paper in my hand. "Petition for what?" she asked.

"Against the highway."

"Petition against the highway?" The woman sneered. "Why would I sign that?"

"Because if the highway gets built, some people will lose their homes. And the people who don't lose their homes will have to put up with a lot of noise and stuff." I tried to sound confident.

The woman wasn't staring anymore. Now she was glaring. "The highway is going ahead. It doesn't matter if a few people are unhappy about it."

I took another deep breath. Was it too late to pretend I'd come to the wrong house?

The woman continued, "And I, for one, can't wait for that highway to be built. It will cut my commute time to Toronto in half. The sooner they get that thing built, the better."

"Oh," I said, suddenly aware that my eyes were stinging.

The woman grabbed the piece of paper still hanging from my outstretched arm. "Haven't had much success?"

"This is my first house."

"Well, good, then," she said, handing back the paper. "Don't waste your time, kid."

I shoved the petition behind me and started to back away. "Okay, well, thanks…"

The woman didn't close the door as I hoped she would. At this point I wouldn't have even minded if she slammed the door in my face. Instead she scowled at me. "Who are you anyway?"

I stopped moving, but I didn't speak. Why had I parked Sonny's bike so far away? It was lying on the manicured lawn, miles from where I now stood. Trembling.

"Are you working for one of those crazy environmental groups?"

"No," I said, "I'm just a...a kid."

"That's pretty low. Getting a kid to go begging door to door." The woman stepped out of the house. I looked down at the plush door mat lying between us. It said *Welcome Friends*.

"I don't know what you're talking about," I stammered.

"Which one is it?" the woman continued. "Greenpeace? The Sierra Club?"

"Neither. None. I'm just here. By myself."

"I don't believe you. Those so-called environmentalists are the only ones still fighting the highway. 'Take the train,'" the woman said in a mocking tone. "'Work from home.' Those green types don't understand a single thing about the real world."

"I really don't know what you're talking about," I said, backing away again. "I'm going to go now. Sorry, I...I bothered you."

"Well, you tell that environmental group of yours that global warming has nothing to do with me and my car," the woman called after me as I made a beeline for Sonny's bike. "It's people like me who keep this economy going. If it wasn't for hard-working people like me…"

She was still talking when I finally reached the bike. I lifted it up and pushed it off the grass, swinging my leg over the seat as fast as I could.

I headed down the front path, swerving to avoid the red SUV parked in the middle of the long driveway. I quickly picked up speed, thankful for the smooth black asphalt that was slick from the heat. So different from the gravel laneways leading up to the other farmhouses.

I didn't slow down until I reached the road. As the cars whipped past me, I stopped and caught my breath. I had a decision to make.

Turning right would lead me directly back to Grandma's. Tempting. I was feeling more than a little discouraged. That woman was crazy! I could collect signatures later. Ask Sonny to come with me. Maybe bribe him with my iPhone.

But what if I couldn't find Sonny? What if he said no? There wasn't much time before Percy Murfin's meeting with Grandma. I could turn left and collect signatures right now. Finish the circuit I'd started, ending with Mrs. Kornitsky's house.

Or were there lots of other people who thought the highway was a good thing?

There was only one way to find out. I wiped the sweat off my face and waited for a break in the traffic. It took a long time.

When I finally saw an opening, I pushed one of the pedals, steering to the left. The bike wobbled, almost spilling me off the side. I steadied myself and pushed again, looking down at the pedals.

HONK!

I looked up to see the car coming toward me.

I pushed again, but the pedal didn't move. Neither did the bike. I knew the chain was jammed, but I couldn't fix it. Not in the middle of the road.

Heart pounding, I stomped my foot down on the pedal as hard as I could.

The bike wobbled and then shot forward.

Just in time.

Before I knew it, I was across both lanes and into the ditch on the other side.

Brushing myself off, I surveyed the cuts on my arms and legs. Nothing life threatening. Just a little blood. Still, I could feel the tears tickling the corners of my eyes.

I picked up the bike. It was in far worse shape than me. I pulled it out of the ditch and stood it up on the side of the road.

The back tire was flat. The seat and the post were no longer attached. And the chain was broken.

Sonny's crappy old bike had made the decision for me. My petition was done.

Chapter Fourteen

It was a long walk back to Grandma's.

By the time I got to the farm, I was beyond discouraged. I was beyond scared. I was hot, hungry and totally miserable.

Pushing Sonny's sad-looking bike up the laneway, all I wanted to do was go to my room, curl up in a ball and stay there until it was time to go home. Back to Cedar Grove.

But I didn't make it. Not to my room. Not even into the farmhouse.

"Bree." I was resting the bike against the garage when I heard Grandma say my name. I was so tired, I hadn't seen her sitting on the front porch. She was in her usual chair. There were two empty glasses on the little table in front of her.

"Grandma?" I took a step closer. A woman I'd never seen before was sitting on the wicker love seat that filled the rest of the front porch. It looked like she was holding a notebook or something.

"We've been waiting for you," Grandma said. "Where have you been?"

"Nowhere special," I said, trying to sound like it didn't matter. I wondered if I looked as awful as I felt.

"Where did you get that?" Grandma said, pointing to the bike.

"I borrowed it from Sonny."

"I didn't know Sonny had a bicycle." Grandma narrowed her eyes at me. "I've never seen him ride it."

"I don't think it gets much use," I replied.

The woman sitting next to Grandma coughed. Loudly.

"Come and meet Ms. Sharp," Grandma said.

As I climbed the stairs from the cracked walkway to the sagging porch, the stranger stood up and stretched her arm out toward me. "Jennifer Sharp."

The Rubik's Cube in my brain clicked into place. This wasn't a stranger. This was Jennifer Sharp. The reporter.

I shook her hand. "Uh, hi?"

"Ms. Sharp came to talk to you." Grandma said this like she was accusing me of wasting well water by taking too long in the shower.

"We spoke on the phone," Ms. Sharp added.

"I remember," I said.

"Do you have time to talk now?" asked Ms. Sharp.

"I guess."

"I'll be inside if you need me," Grandma said, hauling herself up.

"Thank you for your time, Mrs. Bridges." Jennifer Sharp was still standing. She held her hand out to Grandma, who nodded politely but didn't take it.

I wanted to call after Grandma as she disappeared into the farmhouse. I wanted her to stay with me. After the disaster with my petition, I really felt like I was in over my head. Like I was messing with things that were none of my business. The last thing I wanted to do was talk to a reporter.

I opened my mouth and tried to say Grandma's name, but nothing came out. Closing it again, I swallowed hard to try and get rid of the dryness that was spreading down my throat.

Ms. Sharp returned to her perch on the edge of the love seat. I sank into Grandma's chair. It was much more comfortable than it looked.

"I want to do an interview," said Ms. Sharp. She picked up a pen and used it to point to a small digital recorder that was lying on the table in front of her. "I'm going to ask you some questions, and I'd like to record your answers so I can quote you in an article for *The Record*."

"But I thought you weren't interested in the gravesite."

"I'm not," Ms. Sharp replied. "I'm doing an article about the highway development and its effect on the people living in this area."

"You are?" I looked at the empty glasses sitting next to the digital recorder, wishing desperately for a glass of lemonade. This was all a bit confusing, and it was taking my brain a while to catch up. "Why?"

"To be honest, we need some material for the paper. Slow news week, I guess." Ms. Sharp tapped her pen against the notebook in her hand. "When you called me, I realized I had a lead on a good human-interest story."

"Human-interest story?"

"What's happening to you and your grandma."

"Did you talk to her?"

"I did. She didn't give me much. Not much of a talker, your grandma."

I nodded. "But she said it was okay to do the story?"

"She said it was okay that I talk to you."

"That's good…I guess."

"It's going to be a good story. But I'm on a tight deadline, so let's get on with it." Ms. Sharp fiddled with the digital recorder until a red light came on.

"Okay," I said, wondering how I was going to give Jennifer Sharp the information she needed.

"First of all, I need your full name with correct spelling."

Maybe this wasn't going to be so hard after all.

Ms. Sharp's questions didn't get much more complicated than that. As I explained where I lived and how much time I'd spent on the farm and how I'd learned about the highway, I tried to figure out whether this article was a good thing or a bad thing. By the time Ms. Sharp asked me how I felt about it all, I'd decided that the article didn't really matter one way or the other. The highway was going to be built.

And I was going home soon. A newspaper article wasn't going to change a thing.

"Do you need me to repeat the question?" Ms. Sharp said, interrupting my thoughts.

"Uh, yes please," I stammered.

"How do you feel about the highway development?"

"I'm worried about my grandma," I replied honestly. "She's losing her home, and I don't know where she's going to go."

"So that's why you went searching for the convict cemetery?"

"Yes. And that's why I met with Mr. Murfin, and that's why I started this petition." I pulled the crumpled paper out of my short's pocket.

"Oh," Ms. Sharp said as she took the paper from me. "That's good. That's really good."

Jennifer Sharp scribbled so much stuff in her notebook that I was sure it must be full. She asked a bunch more questions about why the petition was blank and whether Percy Murfin had listened to what I had to say. As we got deeper into the story, I started having doubts about it again. Was there stuff I didn't want people to know?

When I'd answered the last of her questions, Ms. Sharp said, "Okay, Brianna, this is all good stuff. I've got to get back to my computer and start writing."

As she stood up to leave, I realized we hadn't talked about Uncle Doug, Sonny, Amber or Jasper. That seemed wrong, since they were part of the story too. But Ms. Sharp hadn't asked any questions about the rest of the family.

"But…"

"Don't worry. You're going to like the article. Your grandma wanted to read it before it's published, but there's not going to be time for that."

"When's it going to be in the paper?"

"Not soon enough, if I don't get going," Ms. Sharp said as she picked up her purse and pulled out her keys. "I've already missed the deadline."

I breathed a sigh of relief. Delay was good. I was more than okay to wait.

Ms. Sharp continued, "So probably not tomorrow but the next day."

My mouth got even drier. Like I'd been chewing on the dusty straw that covered the floor of the chicken coop.

Before disappearing into her car, Ms. Sharp looked me in the eye and said, "Thank you, Brianna. Bree. It's going to be a great article."

"Okay," I said, wanting to believe her.

As I watched her drive down the lane, I felt sick enough to throw up. It was like my empty stomach was suddenly full. Of fear, I guess.

What had I just done? An hour ago I'd decided that I just wanted this whole thing to go away. And now it was going to be in the newspaper. For the whole world to see.

Day after tomorrow. The day I was supposed to fly home.

With any luck, I'd be gone before the paper came out.

Chapter Fifteen

"Why did you let me do it?" I asked as the front door of the farmhouse banged shut behind me. The knob was hanging off the door like a broken branch. I'd done my best to fix it after Percy Murfin's last visit. But it seemed more and more like my best wasn't good enough.

Grandma looked up from her knitting. "Do what?"

"Talk to Ms. Sharp!" I fumed as I filled a glass with water. "She's writing a story for *The Record*, you know!"

"I know," Grandma said calmly, still knitting.

"So you want everyone to read about the highway and what's going to happen to the farm? You don't even like talking about it!" I drained the glass of water and filled it again, trying to ignore the soup bubbling away on the stove. Soup for dinner again? It was still hot outside, even though evening was approaching. The humidity was so heavy and thick, it felt like I was breathing soup. And it wasn't like the farmhouse had air conditioning. I should have offered to do some cooking during my visit, instead of relying on Amber and Grandma.

"I thought it would be good for you to talk about it," Grandma said. "Get it out of your system."

"Get it out of my system?" I was so hot even my ears were burning. "You're losing your home and you want *me* to get it out of *my* system?"

"We can talk about this when you've calmed down a little."

"Fine," I said, annoyed that Grandma wasn't getting mad. If I talked to Mom like that I'd be sentenced to a long time-out. Very long.

I stormed to my room and slammed the door.

As I curled up on my bed, under a comforter covered with rocket ships and planets, the tears started to flow. Now that I was finally in my room—Dad's room actually—I wanted to stay there until it was time to go home. Only two more days.

I didn't even last two minutes.

I was starving. But I didn't want to face Grandma. Or the soup on the stove. So I climbed out the window and went to Amber and Sonny's place, forgetting that it was Uncle Doug's place too.

When I got there, Amber was in the kitchen. As usual.

She looked at me over the pile of laundry she was folding. "Where've you been?" she asked. "I could've used you as a model today. For a dress I'm designing."

"Sorry, I got busy." My stomach let out a huge growl. "What's cooking?"

"Curry," Amber said, crinkling her nose. "New recipe."

"Can't wait to try it," I said. I picked up some laundry and started folding, hoping Amber wouldn't ask any more questions.

"It'll be done soon." Amber looked me up and down. "Tell me what you've been doing. You don't look so good."

"I don't want to talk about it."

"Okay," Amber said with a shrug, "then let's talk about your going-away party."

"Going-away party? What for?"

"Well, aren't you going away?"

"I'm going home." I held up two fingers. "In two days."

"Bet you can't wait," Amber said, a small pout playing on her lower lip. "I wish I was going with you."

"I'd take you with me if I could," I said. I meant it. I was going to miss Amber.

"Sure, sure," Amber said, looking away from me toward the mess on the kitchen table. Jasper was making shapes out of play dough and organizing them into different groups. It seemed pretty random, but knowing Jasper, there had to be a pattern.

"Anyway, about the party," Amber continued.

"I don't need a party."

"Course you do." Amber paused then added, "Grandma's idea."

"Grandma's idea?" I suddenly felt winded and very, very tired. Like I'd just sprinted from Vancouver to Breslau.

"Yup," Amber replied. "She asked me to throw you a big party. Let you know how much we've enjoyed your visit. Then hopefully it won't be so long before you come back."

126

I felt a hundred different things at the same time, like I was under attack by my emotions. I stood there for a minute, holding Uncle Doug's half-folded shirt in my hands, until everything finally spilled over. And out.

With tears rolling down my face again, I told Amber everything. About the petition, the interview and the argument with Grandma. I finished by saying, "I don't know why I didn't listen. Everyone told me the highway couldn't be stopped. They were right. I was wrong."

"But that's what I like most about you, Bree." Amber put her arm around me. "You're so strong. So determined."

"Not determined," I said, drying my tears with the back of my hand. "Stubborn and dumb. The petition idea was just plain stupid."

"No. It was a good idea. But a door-to-door petition is not the way to do things out here in the country. You've got to do it online. When we petitioned for healthy food options at school, we used Facebook. I could've helped—"

Amber was interrupted by the oven timer and Jasper screaming her name at the same time.

Amber rushed over to Jasper. The oven timer continued to buzz.

"Don't worry. We can fix it," Amber said to Jasper as she straightened a tower of play dough with one hand and comforted him by rubbing his back with another. "See? All better." Within a minute, Jasper was back to making cubes and humming quietly to himself as if nothing had happened.

Amber silenced the timer and pulled the curry out of the oven. "Dinner in five. Do you think Grandma's coming?"

Before I had a chance to tell Amber about the soup, she slapped her forehead and said, "Oh no, I forgot to feed the hens."

Watching Amber juggle everything, I suddenly felt even more exhausted. "Don't you get tired of doing everything around here?"

Amber looked at me with surprise. "This is my week to feed them. Sonny's turn to clean the coop."

"It's not just the chickens. You cook, clean, take care of Jasper..." I threw the shirt I was still holding back into the laundry basket. "Why doesn't anyone help?"

"Dad has to work all the time, and Sonny's a nightmare in the house. He helps with the outside stuff," Amber said.

"What about Grandma? She spends all her time helping other people. Why not you? Why not Jasper?"

"Dad doesn't want her helping out."

"Why?"

"They don't get along," Amber replied. "Never have."

"Who? Grandma and Uncle Doug?"

Amber nodded as she started separating the folded laundry into piles. "Haven't you noticed they're hardly ever here at the same time?"

I thought for a minute. It was true. Grandma avoided Uncle Doug as much as I did. Still, it didn't make sense. "Then why did Uncle Doug build your house here?"

"I don't know. It was a difficult time." Amber's face flashed with pain, like she'd just burned her finger on the stove.

A lump formed in my throat as I thought about Aunt Theresa. Any anger that hadn't been washed away by my tears now disappeared. I couldn't imagine losing my mom. "I'm sorry," I said, putting my hand on Amber's arm.

Amber nodded again and then smiled. "I guess Dad thought things between him and Grandma had changed. And he was right for a while. Grandma helped out a lot when Jasper was really little. But then things that Grandma did started driving Dad crazy."

"Things? Like what?"

"If Sonny or I wore holes in the knees of our pants and Grandma sewed on patches, Dad would go out and buy us new pants, and then they'd have a huge fight about it."

"Really?

"I know it doesn't sound like a big deal, but there are lots of examples just like that. They are both so stubborn. Without your dad or my mom around as a buffer, they really just need to keep their distance. Dad says it's the only way to keep things from going really sour between them."

"Oh," I said, feeling embarrassed that I'd misjudged everything. Again.

"I don't know. Maybe things will be easier once this highway is built and we all go our separate ways,"

Amber said as she loaded the piles of laundry back into the basket.

"You really think so?"

Amber didn't answer. Instead, she hauled the laundry off the table and yelled up the stairs, "Sonny! Dinner! Can you feed the hens for me before you come?" Then she cleaned up the play dough and sent Jasper to the bathroom to wash his hands. I helped her set the table.

"I guess we'll talk about your party over dinner," she said.

"Okay," I replied. But really, I just wanted the day to be over.

Chapter Sixteen

"Bree's going home in two days," Amber announced when we were all sitting around the table eating dinner. All of us minus Grandma. The thought of her sitting in the farmhouse alone with her soup made me feel worse than awful.

"Bet you'll be happy to get away from us hicks," Sonny said with a fake drawl.

"Why are you going?" Jasper asked, his mouth full of food.

"I've got to go back for school," I explained.

"Why not school here?" Jasper asked. "Like me. And Sonny. And Amber."

"Bree's school is in Vancouver," Uncle Doug said firmly.

"Why?" Jasper asked again.

"Why, why, why, why, why," Sonny said as he tousled Jasper's hair.

"Bree's mom and dad have jobs in Vancouver," Uncle Doug said. "That's where they've chosen to live." This sounded like an accusation.

"Maybe Bree will come back for a visit again soon. And maybe she'll bring Uncle Steven and Auntie Beth with her," Amber added.

"Uncle Teven and Auntie Bef?" Jasper said, his mouth full again. He was obviously enjoying the curry more than Uncle Doug was.

"Bree's mom and dad," Sonny explained.

Uncle Doug cleared his throat. "I talked to your dad today, in fact."

"You did?" I didn't bother to hide my surprise. "It's been almost a week since he texted me."

"He's been busy wrapping up his business—if you can call it that—in Europe," said Uncle Doug.

"You mean hockey scouting," I said.

"Yes, he's been busy with hockey. He's always been busy with hockey." Uncle Doug looked down at the table as he said the word *hockey*. Like it was something to be embarrassed about.

I sat straight up in my chair. "Dad's now the Director of Hockey Administration for the Vancouver Canucks," I said loudly. Louder than I needed to.

"Yes, I know," Uncle Doug said quickly. "He's planning his trip home so he's back in time to manage training camp."

"He's flying home the same day as me," I said. "Mom's coming to pick us up at the airport."

"Yeah, well," Uncle Doug hesitated.

I jumped in, anxious to know what this was all about. "Well what?"

Uncle Doug cleared his throat. "Your dad told me about the tree-climbing bylaw," he said. "About how you got it overturned."

"You were talking about me?" I dropped my fork. This whole conversation was ruining my appetite. Something I really didn't think was possible.

"We were talking about your summer and..." Uncle Doug hesitated again.

"And what?" I demanded.

"The highway."

The word *highway* hung in the air as everyone finished their curry in silence. I wanted to know more about Uncle Doug's conversation with Dad, but I didn't want to talk about the highway.

When everyone was done eating, Amber started clearing the plates. "So anyway," she said, "we're going to have a bit of a going-away party."

"For who?" Sonny asked.

"Bree." Amber's eyes flashed with annoyance. "Who else?"

"No, I mean who's going to come?" Sonny said with a smile.

"Well...us. And Grandma. Maybe Mrs. Kornitsky."

"Doesn't sound like much of a party," Sonny said, still smiling.

"It'll be fun. I'm going to make lots of good food—"

"But no curry," Uncle Doug interrupted.

Amber continued, ignoring her dad. "We're going to have the party at Grandma's."

"Why?" asked Sonny.

"Why, why, why, why, why," Jasper said, making everyone laugh.

"It's what Grandma wants," Amber said when the laughter had stopped. She looked cautiously at Uncle Doug and then turned to me. "We'll have the party on Friday. The day Bree goes home. What time's your flight?"

"Four," I replied.

"Then we'll have the party over lunch," Amber said. "Everyone has to be there. Friday. Noon."

Everyone nodded in agreement except Uncle Doug. We were all staring at him, waiting for some type of reaction, when he finally stopped playing with his napkin and looked up from the table. Pointing at Jasper, he said, "That kid needs a bath."

"Can you do it, Dad?" Amber asked. "I'm kind of busy here."

By the look on everyone's face, they were as surprised as me.

"How about you, Sonny?" Uncle Doug asked.

"I'm helping Amber," Sonny said, grabbing an empty cup off the table.

"DAD!" Jasper said, his arms outstretched. His hands were as dirty as his face.

"Guess I have no choice," Uncle Doug said, reluctantly picking Jasper up off the chair.

When they were gone, Amber handed Sonny the broom. "I'd like it if you and Dad helped out a little more around here."

"I fed the chickens for you," Sonny said as he started sweeping the floor.

When Sonny's back was turned, Amber gave me a little wink. It made me smile. A little.

Just as Amber, Sonny and I finished cleaning up, Uncle Doug came back into the kitchen. "Jasper's sleeping like a baby," he announced.

"Thanks, Dad," Amber said.

"You don't have to thank me. It was actually kind of fun spending time with him. It's been a while." Uncle Doug sat down at the table, freshly scrubbed by Sonny, although I couldn't help noticing he'd missed a few spots. "What were you saying about Friday at noon?"

"Da-ad!" Amber crinkled her nose. "Bree's party. Friday at noon. Can you please try and be there?"

Uncle Doug sighed. "Some of us have to work, you know."

"Grandma said it was important."

"Well, if *Grandma* says it's important—" Uncle Doug stopped midsentence. "When was that again?"

Amber frowned. "Friday at noon."

"As it turns out, I'm taking Friday afternoon off anyway."

"Why?" Sonny asked. He was standing in the doorway, obviously anxious to get to his room, but curiosity seemed to be holding him back.

"I have a meeting," Uncle Doug responded.

"Meeting?" Sonny asked. "Where?"

"Here. At the farm."

"With who?" asked Sonny.

"Mr. Murfin."

As soon as I heard Uncle Doug say Percy Murfin's name, I knew I had to get out. Out of the kitchen, off the farm and away from Ontario.

This had been, without a doubt, the longest day of my life.

Chapter Seventeen

I spent the next day packing. It didn't take long. After that, I climbed each of the trees I'd gotten to know over the summer. That took longer. Saying goodbye to the trees was hard. I tried not to think about what was going to happen to them when the highway was built.

I was climbing Skeleton, one of the trees over-looking the convict cemetery, when I heard Sonny calling my name.

"Up here!" I yelled in the general direction of his voice.

"What are you doing?" Sonny asked when he reached the base of the tree.

"Climbing," I replied as I pulled myself higher.

"Why here?"

"Why not?"

"I've been looking everywhere for you," Sonny said. "Can I come up?"

"It's not my tree," I said with a smile.

I stopped climbing and waited for him. When he reached the branch below me, I started up the tree again, searching for a place to rest. Somewhere with a level branch and a view.

"Where are you going?" Sonny called from below. "I want to talk to you!"

I kept going until I found an okay spot. There wasn't really enough room for two, but I didn't think it was safe to go much higher. "Talk about what?" I asked as I settled into the tree.

Sonny didn't reply until he was awkwardly perched on the branch next to mine. "This," he said, reaching toward the back pocket of his jeans. Tugging with one hand, he let go of the branch he was sitting on and twisted to look behind him. Worried he was going to lose his balance, I reached out and grabbed his shoulder.

He turned back so we were facing each other again. He was holding a newspaper. I dropped my hand. I think I might have even gasped. *The Record*.

"You're famous," Sonny said.

My stomach flipped. I'd done such a good job of focusing on going home that I'd almost forgotten about that stupid article. Plus, I didn't expect it in the paper until tomorrow. Until I was back in Vancouver.

"Let me see," I said, reaching for the paper.

Sonny whipped the paper away from me and held it above his head. "Not so fast."

I moved my legs so I was crouching on my branch instead of sitting. "Come on," I said.

"Why are you so worried?" Sonny asked.

"I want to know what it says!"

"Don't worry," Sonny said. "It's a good article."

"Let me see!" I was on my feet, my fingertips almost touching the newspaper.

"It mentions Grandma," Sonny said, "but none of us."

"So?" I couldn't tell if Sonny thought that was good or bad.

"It made me realize that I should've said something. A long time ago." Sonny was still holding the paper over his head, but he wasn't teasing anymore. He was serious. "How did you manage to get so much attention, Bree?"

"I thought the highway was wrong," I said, "so I spoke up." I lunged forward, trying to grab the newspaper with my free hand.

Sonny pulled the newspaper behind his back. "You make it sound like no big deal."

"That's because it's not," I said, lunging toward him again.

"It is a big deal," Sonny said, pulling away from me. Away from the trunk.

I was so desperate to get the newspaper that I didn't really hear the compliment.

But I did hear the crack.

We were too high. The branches up here were too thin.

Before I realized what was happening, Sonny lost his balance.

There wasn't much I could do, standing in the tree with one hand on the trunk and the other reaching forward. All I could do was watch as Sonny fell from the branch that had split away from the trunk.

All the way to the ground.

Chapter Eighteen

"This isn't exactly the party I had planned," Amber said. She was shuffling around Sonny's hospital bed handing out sandwiches. Egg salad.

Sonny laughed. "Ouch!" he said, grabbing at his side. "It hurts to laugh."

Amber reached around the cast on Sonny's leg to move the bed into a sitting position. "Stay still," she instructed.

In addition to his leg, Sonny had broken three ribs. Even the tiniest movement was painful for him, and the doctor said it was going to hurt for a while. But at least the bones would heal. Sonny would be okay, something I really hadn't been sure of when I ran to Mrs. Kornitsky's house after he fell. I'd gone to get help, leaving Sonny in a heap on the ground, not wanting to move him in case I hurt him even more. The thought still made me shudder.

"Food's good," Sonny said as he bit into the sandwich. "Even if the rest of the party's a bit of a downer."

"What part?" I asked. "The fact that you're in the hospital or the lack of guests?" I put down the pillow I was holding between my chair and Sonny's bed so I could take a sandwich from Amber.

"Hey! My bridge!" said Jasper. The pillow had been part of his pretend town.

"Time to put the cars away and eat some lunch," Amber said as she reached out and pulled Jasper into her lap.

"I want Bree!" Jasper said, crawling onto my chair.

My dark mood lightened slightly. It was the first time I'd heard Jasper say my name all summer. At least someone was sad to see me go. But I still felt awful. "I'm so sorry, Sonny."

"It's not your fault, Bree," Sonny said for the hundredth time. "I'm the one who fell out of the tree."

"But I broke my own rule. We shouldn't have been up that high. The branches were too thin…"

"It was me who was goofing around," Sonny mumbled through his mouthful of food.

"Still—"

"Where's Daddy?" interrupted Jasper.

"He's probably still at work," Sonny said. "He'll be here."

Uncle Doug had stayed at the hospital overnight. He said he didn't trust the doctors, but I think Sonny's fall had really scared him. According to Sonny, he'd left for work early in the morning, promising to be back in time for the party.

"Dad being late doesn't surprise me," Amber said, "but where's Grandma? This party was her idea."

Amber, Jasper and I had come to the hospital with Grandma a couple of hours ago. But Grandma had disappeared almost immediately, claiming she had to visit a friend who was recovering from hip replacement surgery.

A nurse came in to check on Sonny while we were finishing our sandwiches. "Time for your one-o'clock meds," she announced.

My plane left in three hours. I had no idea who was going to take me to the airport. We were at Grand River Hospital in Kitchener, which was a lot farther away from Waterloo International Airport than the farm.

"I made you something," Amber said to me when the nurse was gone.

I took the package. It was as perfectly wrapped as the one she'd given me for my birthday.

"I'll open it!" Jasper said. He neatly unfolded the paper that most other five-year-olds would have torn apart.

Inside was a shirt with one of Amber's silk-screen designs on it. It was the silhouette of a chicken standing in the middle of a wide road. Underneath, in small letters, it said *Road Block.*

A huge smile spread across my face. "I love it!" Taking a closer look at the fabric, I added, "It matches the skirt you gave me for my birthday."

Amber crinkled her nose. "I've figured out that you're not much of a skirt girl," she said.

"Doesn't matter," I said, holding up the shirt for Sonny to see. "Now I have two original Amber Bridges designs."

"Nice job, sis," Sonny said. "That shirt is perfect for Bree."

Amber's cheeks turned pink as she smiled. "Thanks."

"Daddy!' Jasper yelled.

I was sitting with my back to the door. I didn't want to wreck any more of Jasper's car town so I didn't move. But I was glad Uncle Doug had arrived. Maybe he could take me to the airport.

Then I heard Amber say, "Uncle Steve?"

I whipped my head around, forgetting all about Jasper's town. "Dad?"

There wasn't much space left in Sonny's room, so I had to wait patiently as Dad worked his way toward me. "Hi, Amber. How're you feeling, Sonny? You're so big, Jasper!"

When he finally reached my chair, I stood up and hugged him. "Dad!"

"Bree," he said into my shoulder, hugging me so hard my feet came off the ground.

"What are you doing here?" I asked when he released me.

"I missed you too," Dad said with a laugh.

"That's not what I meant!"

"I know," Dad said, glancing at Uncle Doug. "I thought it would be nice to spend a little time with my family before the summer is over."

"But I'm leaving in less than three hours," I said.

"No, you're not," Dad replied. "I changed your flight."

"What?"

"We're going to spend the weekend here," Dad explained, "and fly home together on Sunday. I hope you don't mind."

"I...I guess not," I said. I wasn't sure what else to say. Everything was changing so fast.

Amber laughed. "Now this going away party is an official bust. You're not even going away!"

"Not yet!" I smiled, glad that Amber was excited, even though I was feeling overwhelmed by the change of plan. Now I was going to have to wait even longer to see Sarah. And Michael. And Mom.

"Sorry we're late," Uncle Doug said to Amber. "Uncle Steve's flight was a few minutes delayed and the traffic was bad."

"I didn't even know you were going to the airport!" said Amber.

"You didn't say anything about it when you left this morning," Sonny added.

Uncle Doug picked up the chart hanging from the end of Sonny's bed. "I didn't know myself until Grandma called and told me I had to pick up your Uncle Steve."

"It was a last-minute thing," Dad said. "Where's Grandma?"

"No idea," Sonny said. "She's been gone for hours."

"Is that usual?" Dad asked, raising his eyebrows at Uncle Doug.

"Grandma does a lot of volunteer work at the hospital," I said. "She probably ran into someone she knew."

"Does she know you're coming?" Sonny asked my dad.

Dad nodded. "It was her idea."

"It was?" I asked.

"She said she wanted her family together."

"You talked to her?" I asked. Grandma sure had been busy. How had I not noticed?

"Every day since you arrived," Dad replied.

What?

"So you know all about Bree's fight against the highway?" Sonny asked, pulling yesterday's newspaper off the table next to him.

"Of course," Dad said. "Bree spent the summer being Bree."

"It's been awesome having her here," Amber said.

"I'm glad you've gotten to know each other again," Dad said. "It's been too long."

I stood there waiting for my brain to catch up as Dad read the article in the paper and Uncle Doug read Sonny's chart. The room was silent, apart from the sound of Jasper honking and zooming his cars around the room.

All of a sudden, the door flew open. Grandma. "Oh good, you're all here," she said. Behind her was Percy Murfin.

Sonny's hospital room was now full to overflowing.

This was about to become a real party.

Chapter Nineteen

Uncle Doug was the first to welcome our surprise visitor. "I'm sorry about our meeting, Percy."

Percy Murfin coughed nervously. "Well, actually—"

"There'll be no need for any more meetings," Grandma interrupted. "Mr. Murfin and I have reached an agreement."

Everyone in the room gasped. Even Jasper. Although Jasper's gasp was just a sound effect for one of his cars running out of gas.

"What?" Sonny said as he bent forward in his bed. Then, "Ouch!"

"How are you feeling, Sonny?" Grandma asked, ignoring the fact that she had everyone's attention.

Sonny groaned.

"Hi, Mom," Dad said, reaching across the bed to give Grandma a hug.

"Steven." Grandma patted Dad on the cheek, avoiding his embrace. "I'd like you to meet Percy Murfin. Mr. Murfin, this is my youngest son, Steven. I believe you've met everyone else?"

"I believe so," said Percy Murfin, looking around the room as he shook Dad's hand. "Sorry to hear about your fall, Sonny boy."

Sonny frowned. It was obvious he did not like Percy Murfin. Probably even less than I did.

"Do you mind explaining what this is all about?" Uncle Doug asked Percy Murfin.

"I'll do the explaining," Grandma interjected. "Mr. Murfin is here in case any of you have questions I can't answer."

We all turned toward Grandma. Even Jasper, who was now lining up his cars at Uncle Doug's feet.

"Mr. Murfin and I just completed our meeting in the hospital cafeteria," Grandma said. "The farm has been saved."

I felt like a marionette whose strings had just been cut.

"You stopped the highway?" Sonny gasped.

"No, the highway will still be built," Grandma replied. "But it won't be running through the farmhouse."

"The highway's been rerouted? That's great!" Uncle Doug clapped and rubbed his hands together. Pointing at Percy Murfin, he said, "I'm sure we can come to a reasonable financial agreement for the portion of land the province needs to purchase."

"The province will not be expropriating any of your family's land, Doug," Percy Murfin replied.

The smile disappeared from Uncle Doug's face. "What?"

"The highway has been rerouted to the edge of your property line," Percy Murfin explained. "You get to keep the land. All of it."

Amber put her hands to her cheeks. "And our house?"

"The new routing puts the highway next to your land, but far enough from the houses that there shouldn't be too much noise. We're also going to put in a soundproof fence."

"What about Mrs. Kornitsky?" I asked.

"A soundproof fence will also be incorporated into the construction plan for her property. As well as a concrete driveway."

It was Amber who said exactly what I was thinking. "That's great!"

Uncle Doug's mouth was open, but so far nothing had come out.

"This makes sense to me," said Dad. "You're disturbing fewer landowners. Why didn't you route it that way in the first place?"

Percy Murfin reached into his briefcase. "This is actually going to cost us a lot more. We have to build the fence, move multiple pipelines, construct a new overpass—"

"Then why are you doing it?" Uncle Doug interrupted. "Why not follow the route I suggested? It would save so much money!"

"We had no choice," Percy Murfin replied, looking at me. "The public pressure was too great."

"Thanks to Bree," Grandma added.

"Me?" I blurted out in surprise. "Why me?"

"After the interview you and your grandma gave to *The Record*, our office was flooded with phone calls."

"Phone calls?" I repeated, swallowing hard. "What phone calls?"

"Complaints from other people who will be affected by the highway. Concern from people who were touched by your story. They all wanted to make sure you and the other families around here were treated fairly."

"They were?" I couldn't believe it. The article was good, not at all embarrassing like I thought it might be, but I didn't think it was that good. "They did?"

"The public spoke, and we were forced to listen," said Percy Murfin. "I just wish it had happened sooner, during the initial consultation pro—"

Uncle Doug didn't let him finish. "But I have been—I mean my family has been—fighting from the beginning. You're only listening to us now because an election is coming up."

Percy Murfin put his hands up in front of his chest as if Uncle Doug had aimed a gun at his heart. "Not everyone is going to be happy with this change. Construction will be delayed until the new drawings are completed. A lot of people rely on this transportation corridor, and we need to get it running efficiently. Sooner rather than later."

"It's impossible to please everyone," Dad said slowly, choosing his words carefully as usual. "But this sounds like a good compromise."

"This is awesome!" Sonny said.

"What's awesome?" asked Jasper.

"We don't have to move." Amber jumped up to hug me.

Dad squeezed my shoulder and smiled at Grandma. "You get to keep your home "

Grandma shook her head. "The land will stay in the family. But I'm moving."

There was another gasp, and then the room fell silent. As if we were all trying to make sense of what Grandma had just said.

Percy Murfin was collecting his things. No one had looked at the map or any of the other paperwork he'd taken out of his briefcase. Not even Uncle Doug. He was still holding Sonny's hospital chart.

"If we're finished here, Mrs. Bridges, I should get back to the office."

"We're done," Grandma said. "Thank you, Mr. Murfin."

Percy Murfin extended his hand. Grandma clasped it, reluctantly. Then he shook hands with Dad and Uncle Doug. "Good day, Bridges. Enjoy your land. Convict cemetery and all," he said, winking at me.

And then he was gone.

Chapter Twenty

With Percy Murfin out of the room, Uncle Doug finally let go of Sonny's chart and sat down at the end of the hospital bed with his head between his hands.

"Do you have any more of those sandwiches, Amber?" Grandma said, pointing at the crumbs and crusts Jasper had left sitting on the little table next to Sonny's bed.

"Of course," Amber said, digging through the cooler she'd packed with food and drinks for the party.

Grandma collapsed in the empty chair next to me as Amber handed out a second round of sandwiches.

"Thanks, Amber, I'm starving," Dad said, smiling as he unwrapped his sandwich.

I chewed on the straw of my juice box, trying to figure out what had just happened.

"Are you really moving, Grandma?" Sonny finally dared to ask.

Grandma nodded, chewing slowly.

"That's quite the bomb you just dropped," said Dad. "You've got to fill us in. When are you moving, Mom? Where?"

Grandma didn't respond until she was done eating. "Not sure," she said, opening her purse. She seemed so relaxed, I thought she was going to pull out her knitting. I was wrong. It was a sales brochure. "I want to buy a condo in this new development. I'm hoping you'll all come and take a look at it with me this weekend."

"You think you'll be happy in a condo?" Dad said, looking at the brochure. "You've been on the farm a long time."

"Bree tells me you like living in Cedar Grove, with lots of friends close at hand," Grandma replied. "I'm hoping I can find a condo with a garden and a couple of extra bedrooms so there's room for you to stay. I really want my son and his family to visit me more often."

"Me too," I said.

"Me too," Amber said.

"Me three!" said Jasper.

Everyone laughed. Except Uncle Doug.

"And I'm going to plan a trip out to Vancouver," Grandma continued. "It's about time I saw that town-house of yours."

Uncle Doug looked up. "And how are you going to pay for all this?"

"The condos aren't that expensive," said Grandma, handing Uncle Doug the brochure. "And I've saved a lot of the money from renting out the land and barn."

"How nice for you." Uncle Doug smirked. "But what about us?"

"We can discuss the details later, Doug," Dad said.

Uncle Doug shot Dad a nasty look. "Easy for you to say. You live across the country. None of this affects you the way it affects me."

"Doesn't this mean you can develop the land?" I asked, not wanting to hear Uncle Doug argue with Dad. "Isn't that what you wanted?"

"Development requires money. Something I don't have if the province isn't buying any land."

"But we have our house," Amber said.

"A crappy house on a useless piece of land," Uncle Doug muttered under his breath.

"Not useless," Grandma said. "The land is worth a lot of money. Whether it remains a farm or gets developed into something else."

Uncle Doug looked up at the ceiling. "According to who?"

"According to my lawyers," Grandma replied, still calm. "They had it assessed."

"I didn't know you had lawyers involved, Mom." Dad was still standing next to Grandma's chair. "Why?" he asked.

"I'm giving the land to you and your brother," Grandma answered. "The lawyers just completed the paperwork. You and Doug own the land now. You're smart boys. I'm sure you'll figure out what to do with it."

"You're leaving it to us?" Uncle Doug looked confused.

"I'm hoping we'll get along better with a bit of space between us. And I'm hoping you can focus on your family now that this highway business has been dealt with."

Uncle Doug crossed his arms over his chest.

"We'll take good care of the land," Dad said. "Promise."

"The land doesn't really matter anymore. As long as you do what's best for the family. For my grand-children." Grandma's eyes moved around the room, connecting with each of us. "I want you all to be able to pursue your dreams. Organic farming. Fashion design. Car racing. Whatever." When she stopped talking, she was looking at me.

Warmth spread over me, like hot chocolate sauce being poured on ice cream. "Thank you, Grandma," I said.

"Thank *you*, Bree," Grandma replied, "for reminding me of what's important. Believe it or not, I was a lot like you when I was eleven."

"Twelve," Dad said, placing his hand on the top of my head like the cherry on top of a sundae. "I think you grew this summer!"

"We all did," Grandma said.

Uncle Doug got up from Sonny's bed and headed toward the door. "I'm going to talk to the doctor," he announced.

"Talk to the doctor about what?" Sonny asked.

"Getting you outta here," Uncle Doug replied. "Bree's only going to be here a couple more days. I don't think any of us want to spend the time cooped up in a hospital."

I felt a rush of excitement as I thought about going back to the farm with Dad. It was just a couple more days, but I'd be back again.

Uncle Doug still didn't look very happy, but everyone else in the room did. Including Grandma. And that was enough for me.

Acknowledgments

This story was inspired by the land my grandma has lived on most of her life. My thanks to her, my grandpa, my mom and the entire Demartin clan for giving me wonderful memories of the farm. Although *Road Block* is a work of fiction, Bree's experiences would not have been possible if it wasn't for all of you.

Thank you also to my wonderful critique group, In the Middle Critters (Miriam Franklin, Stephanie Gorin, Karen B. Schwartz, Rachel Cole and David Wright), who helped make the editing for this book much easier than the first. And many, many thanks to Orca Book Publishers (Sarah Harvey, Andrew Wooldridge, Leslie Bootle and everyone working behind the scenes) for doing such a wonderful job with *Trouble in the Trees* that I just had to work with you again.

Finally, I am blessed with a wonderful network of friends and family who have supported me unconditionally. I am extremely grateful for all of you, especially Tim, Oliver and Spencer. Thank you.

Yolanda Ridge's first novel about the irrepressible Bree Bridges was *Trouble in the Trees*. She also writes poetry for children of all ages. She lives four blocks from the highway in a small town in the mountains of British Columbia. Visit www.yolandaridge.com for more information.